MUNCHKIN®

VOLUME ONE

A catalog record of this book is available from OCLC and from the BOOM! Studios website, www.boom-studios.com, on the Librarians page.

BOOM! Studios, 5670 Wilshire Boulevard, Suite 450, Los Angeles, CA 90036-5679. Printed in China. First Printing.

ISBN-13: 978-1-60886-782-0 eISBN: 978-1-61398-453-6

MUNCHKIN®

WRITTEN BY
TOM SIDDELL

ILLUSTRATED BY
MIKE HOLMES
(CHAPTERS 1,4)
AND IAN MCGINTY
(CHAPTERS 2,3)

COLORS BY
FRED STRESING

"MUNCHKIN MINIS"
WRITTEN BY
JIM ZUB
ILLUSTRATED BY
RIAN SYGH

LETTERS BY
JIM CAMPBELL

"TABLE OF CONTENTS"
WRITTEN AND ILLUSTRATED BY
JOHN KOVALIC
COLORS BY KATY FARINA

DESIGNER
KARA LEOPARD

ASSOCIATE EDITOR
JASMINE AMIRI

EDITOR
SHANNON WATTERS

SPECIAL THANKS TO STEVE JACKSON, PHIL REED, ANDREW HACKARD AND ALL OF THE AMAZING FOLKS AT STEVE JACKSON GAMES.

CHAPTER ONE

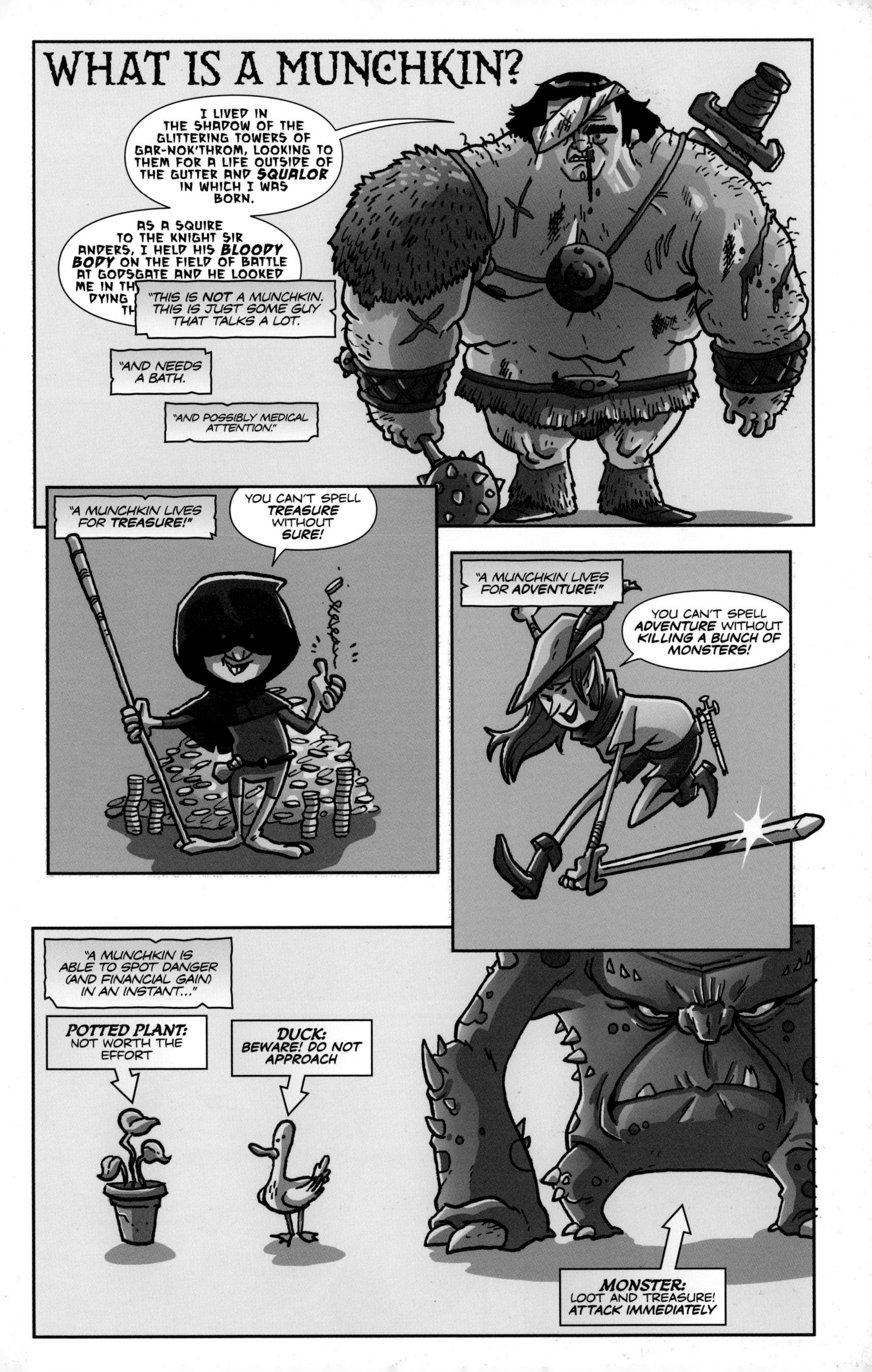
WHAT IS A MUNCHKIN?
I LIVED IN THE SHADOW OF THE GLITTERING TOWERS OF GAR-NOK'THROM, LOOKING TO THEM FOR A LIFE OUTSIDE OF THE GUTTER AND SQUALOR IN WHICH I WAS BORN.
AS A SQUIRE TO THE KNIGHT SIR ANDERS, I HELD HIS BLOODY BODY ON THE FIELD OF BATTLE AT GODSGATE AND HE LOOKED
"THIS IS NOT A MUNCHKIN. THIS IS JUST SOME GUY THAT TALKS A LOT.
"AND NEEDS A BATH.
"AND POSSIBLY MEDICAL ATTENTION."
"A MUNCHKIN LIVES FOR TREASURE!"
YOU CAN'T SPELL TREASURE WITHOUT SURE!
"A MUNCHKIN LIVES FOR ADVENTURE!"
YOU CAN'T SPELL ADVENTURE WITHOUT KILLING A BUNCH OF MONSTERS!
"A MUNCHKIN IS ABLE TO SPOT DANGER (AND FINANCIAL GAIN) IN AN INSTANT..."
POTTED PLANT: NOT WORTH THE EFFORT
DUCK: BEWARE! DO NOT APPROACH
MONSTER: LOOT AND TREASURE! ATTACK IMMEDIATELY

"TO A MUNCHKIN, TEAMWORK IS ESSENTIAL..."

"HOW **ELSE** COULD YOU BETRAY YOUR TEAMMATES FOR MORE LOOT?!"

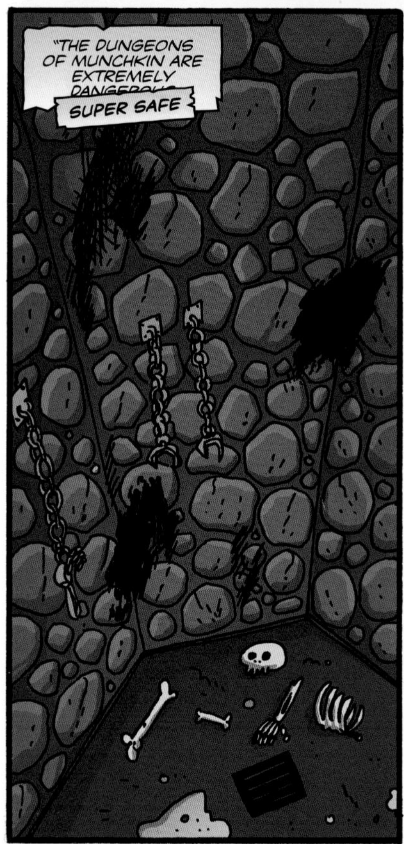
"THE DUNGEONS OF MUNCHKIN ARE EXTREMELY
SUPER SAFE

"WHILE YOU MAY FIND RICHES BEYOND YOUR WILDEST DREAMS...

"YOU MAY ALSO FIND YOUR
TONS OF LOOT AND GOOD TIMES AND FRIENDS

"IF YOU CHOOSE TO ENTER THE DUNGEON, YOU HEARBY ABSOLVE YOUR RIGHT TO--"

SO, YOUNG ADVENTURERS. WHAT DO YOU SAY?

SO WHAT YOU'RE SAYING IS, IF WE GO INTO THE DUNGEON, WE'LL GET RICH...
...AND THERE ARE NO CONSEQUENCES?

CORRECT...

NO CONSEQUENCES WHATSOEVER.
THIS IS THE BEST DECISION WE'VE MADE ALL DAY!
-END-

HUMANS GOT NO CLASS
FOR ADVENTURE!
FOR KNOWLEDGE.
FOR RICHES!
OKAY, GUYS, YEAH! FOR WHATEVER.

YOW! LOOK AT THAT!
WHAT? WHAT HAPPENED?!
STAB!
SLAM
POW
LOOK OUT!

WHAT DID YOU FIND?

THIS COIN!

LOOK AT THIS COIN! IT'S LIKE NEW!

I BET THIS CAME STRAIGHT FROM THE MINT! I BET IT WAS MADE THIS YEAR!

NOPE... NOPE... IT WAS MADE LAST YEAR.

BUT STILL!

IT'S SO GREAT TO SEE A NICE, SHINY COIN. IT'S LIKE A BREATH OF FRESH AIR, SINCE YOU NORMALLY JUST GET THE USUAL DULL KINDS, RIGHT?

I CAN DEFINITELY SAY THIS IS THE **BEST** COIN I'VE EVER SEEN...
...ALL WEEK.
POSSIBLY THE PAST **TWO** WEEKS!

...OKAY, OKAY. THE PAST WEEK AND A HALF, FOR **SURE.**
SO COOL.

YOU FOOL! DON'T YOU SEE ALL THE RICHES AROUND YOU?!
HAHA! NEAT!

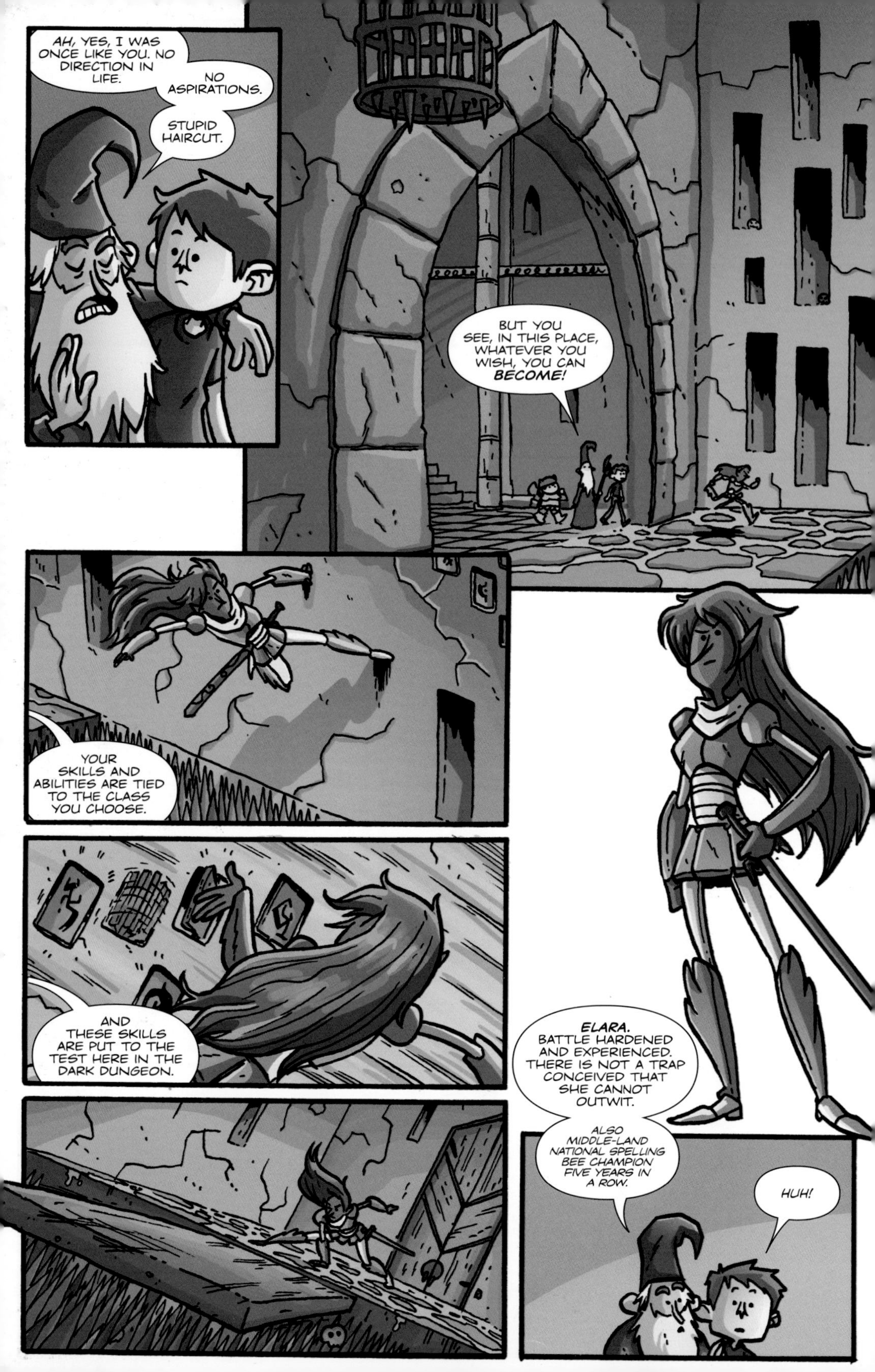
AH, YES, I WAS ONCE LIKE YOU. NO DIRECTION IN LIFE.
NO ASPIRATIONS.
STUPID HAIRCUT.
BUT YOU SEE, IN THIS PLACE, WHATEVER YOU WISH, YOU CAN BECOME!
YOUR SKILLS AND ABILITIES ARE TIED TO THE CLASS YOU CHOOSE.
AND THESE SKILLS ARE PUT TO THE TEST HERE IN THE DARK DUNGEON.
ELARA. BATTLE HARDENED AND EXPERIENCED. THERE IS NOT A TRAP CONCEIVED THAT SHE CANNOT OUTWIT.
ALSO MIDDLE-LAND NATIONAL SPELLING BEE CHAMPION FIVE YEARS IN A ROW.
HUH!

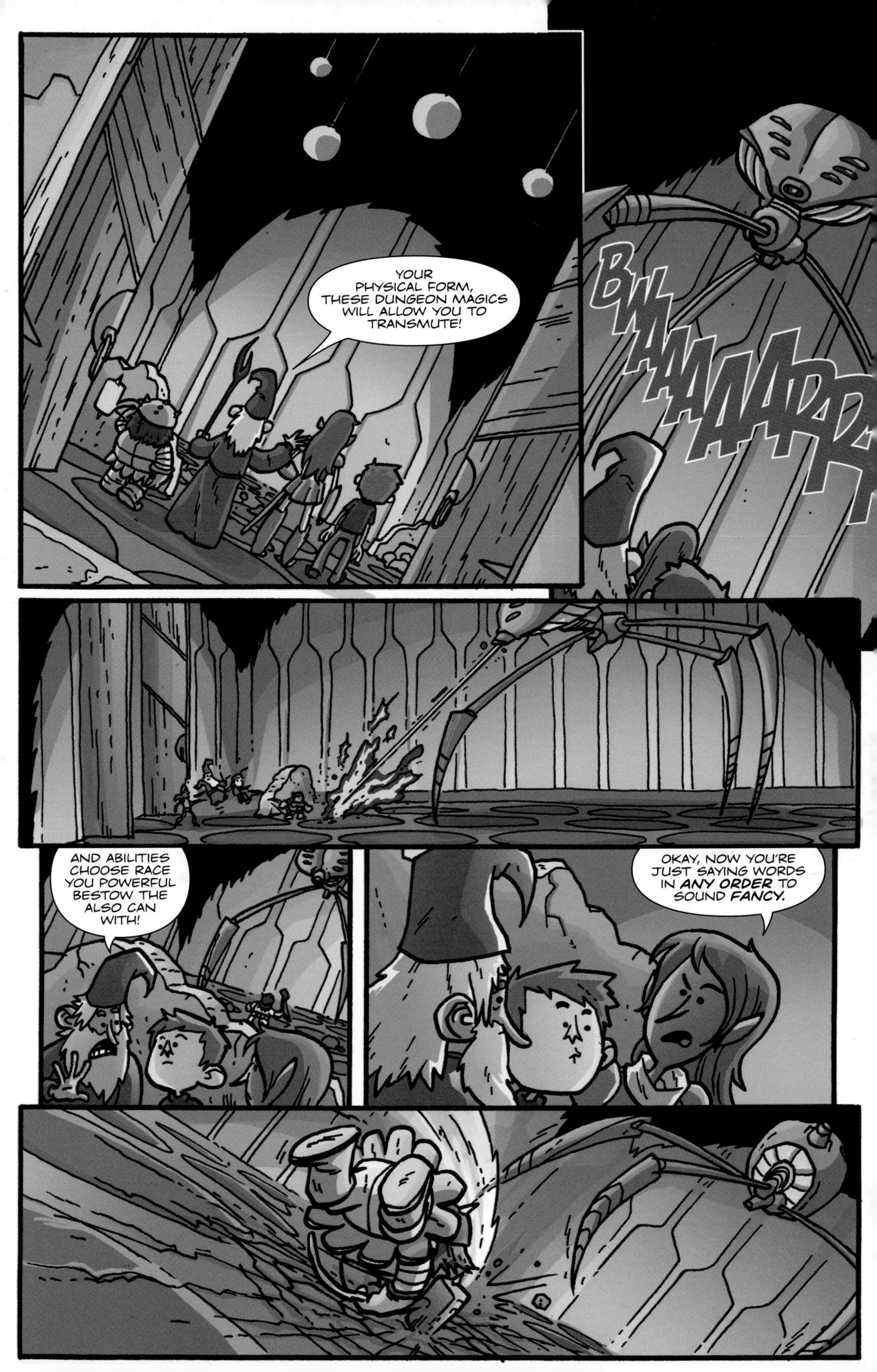
YOUR PHYSICAL FORM, THESE DUNGEON MAGICS WILL ALLOW YOU TO TRANSMUTE!
BWAAAAARRR
AND ABILITIES CHOOSE RACE YOU POWERFUL BESTOW THE ALSO CAN WITH!
OKAY, NOW YOU'RE JUST SAYING WORDS IN ANY ORDER TO SOUND FANCY.

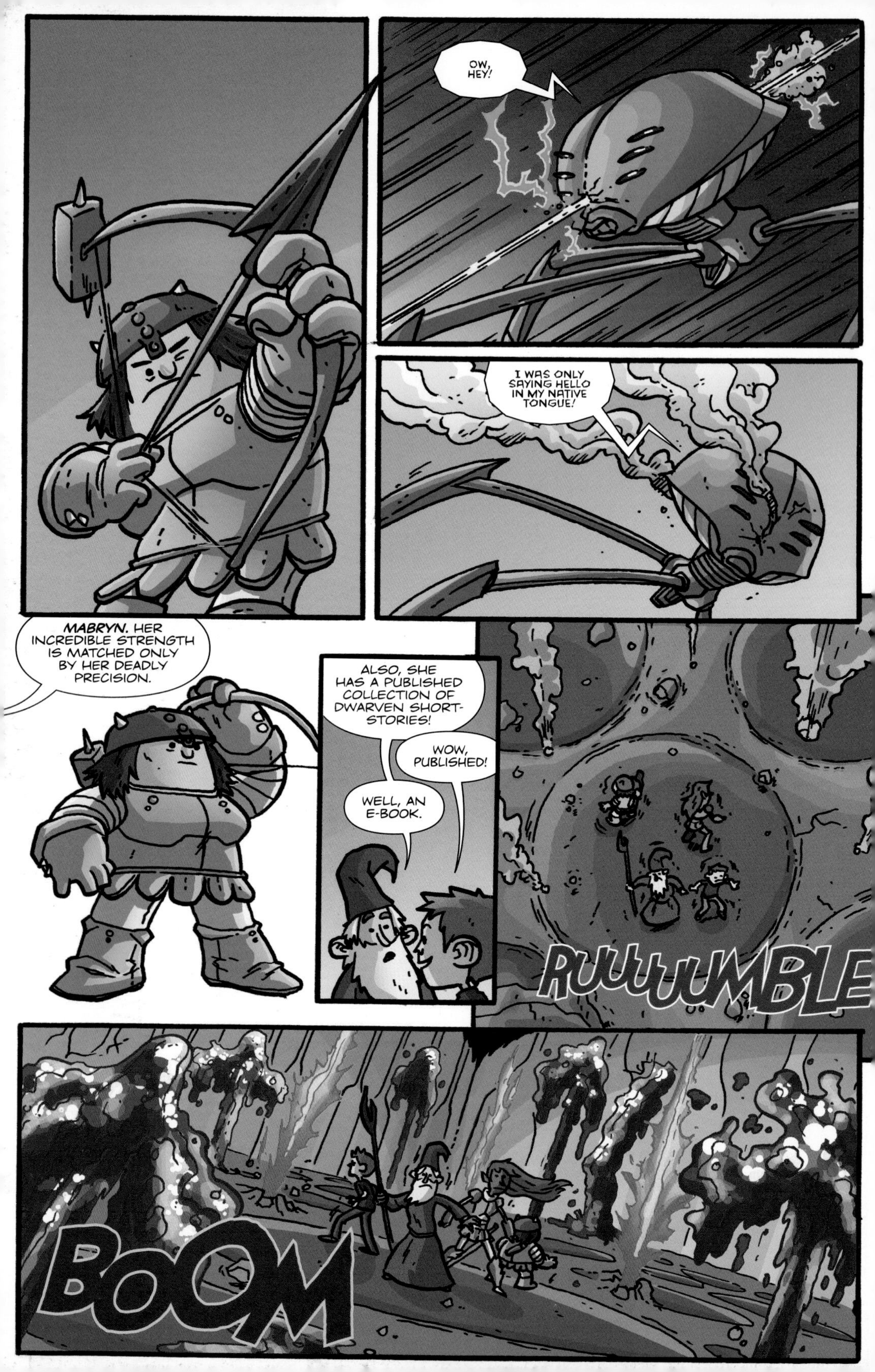
OW, HEY!
I WAS ONLY SAYING HELLO IN MY NATIVE TONGUE!
MABRYN. HER INCREDIBLE STRENGTH IS MATCHED ONLY BY HER DEADLY PRECISION.
ALSO, SHE HAS A PUBLISHED COLLECTION OF DWARVEN SHORT-STORIES!
WOW, PUBLISHED!
WELL, AN E-BOOK.
RUUUUUMBLE
BOOM

AND I, CEDRONK, ONCE A MERE HUMAN LIKE YOURSELF...
(WITH BETTER HAIR)
...CAN BECOME AN ARCANE MASTER, BENDING THE WORLD TO HIS WILL!
WITH OVER THREE HUNDRED TWITTER FOLLOWERS!
HAHA! CEDRONK?

AND SO, HAVE YOU...

DAVE.
DAVE! DAVE, THE HUMAN. HAVE YOU CONSIDERED YOUR DESTINY?
NOPE. NOT FEELIN' IT!

WHY YOU LITTLE--

RUUUMMBLE

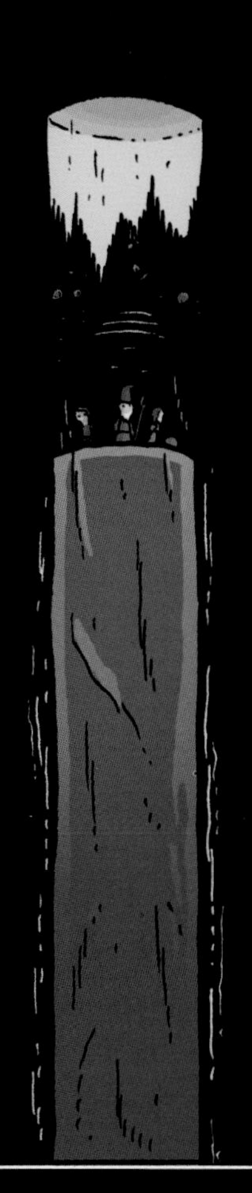

YOU REALLY CAN'T THINK OF **ANY** SKILLS YOU WANT?

WELL, I WAS THINKING OF TAKING A YEAR OFF AFTER COLLEGE...

...BUT I GUESS I'D HAVE TO GO TO COLLEGE FIRST.

YOU WERE INTERESTED IN THAT COIN YOU FOUND.

THAT WAS A REALLY COOL COIN...

RICHES, THEN! YOU CAN ADVENTURE SOLELY FOR WEALTH AND PERSONAL GAIN!

UMM, EXCUSE ME, BUT MONEY DOES NOT BUY YOU HAPPINESS.
WORKS FOR ME!

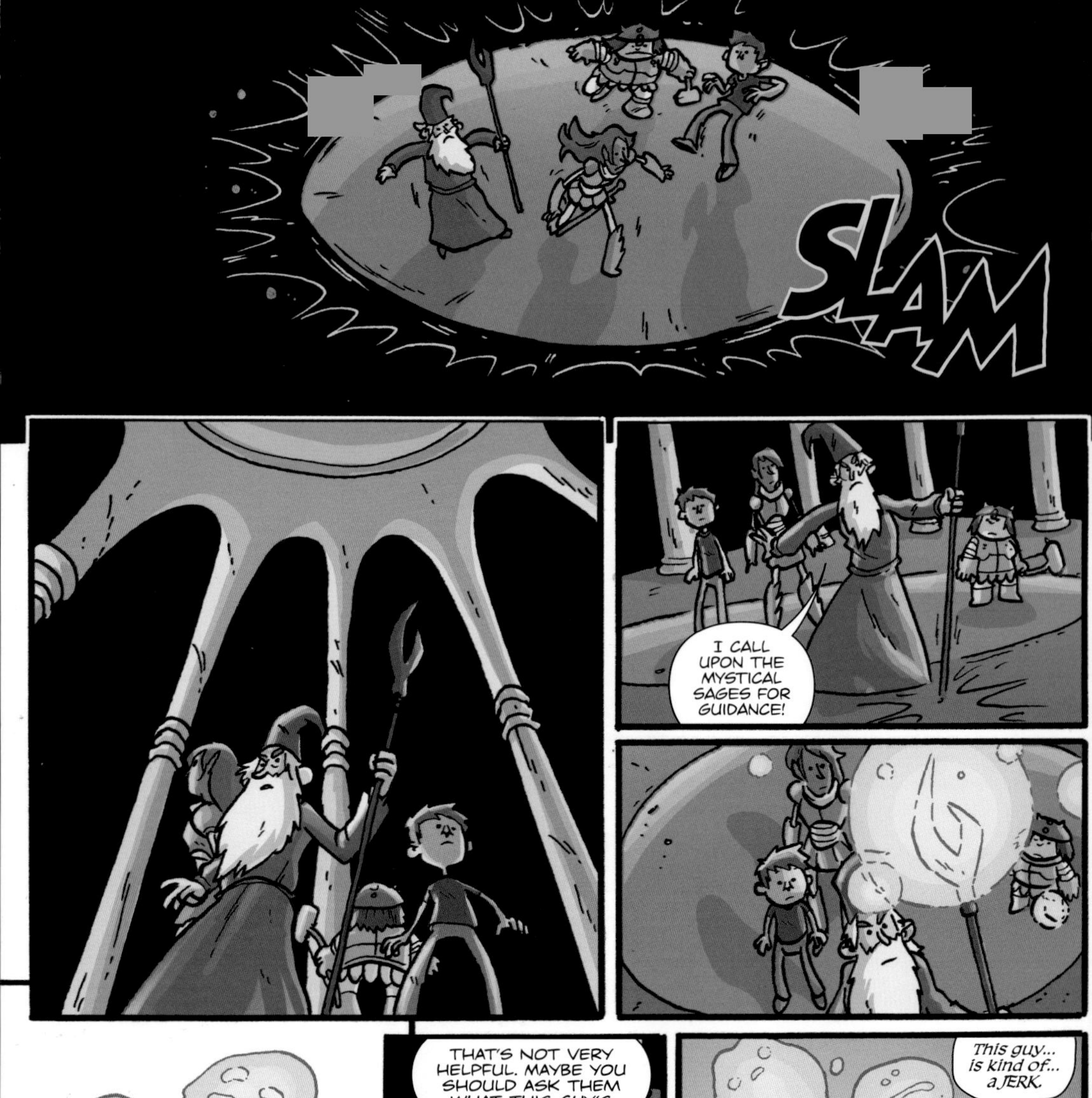
SLAM
I CALL UPON THE MYSTICAL SAGES FOR GUIDANCE!

Through one of these doors lies the Dungeon's END. But make a WRONG CHOICE, and to the FIERY DEPTHS you will descend.

THAT'S NOT VERY HELPFUL. MAYBE YOU SHOULD ASK THEM WHAT THIS GUY'S DEAL IS.

This guy... is kind of... a JERK.

'SPLAINS IT!
HAHA!

HAHAHAHAHA!
IT TURNS OUT I MIGHT HAVE ONE HIDDEN SKILL AFTER ALL!
A-HA! A TURNCOAT! I SHOULD HAVE EXPECTED NO LESS!
BACK-STABBERY IS PERHAPS THE OLDEST SKILL OF ALL!
SO, THE DUNGEON HAS FINALLY REVEALED YOUR TWISTED, INNER-SELF!
NAH. I JUST OWN THE GAME.

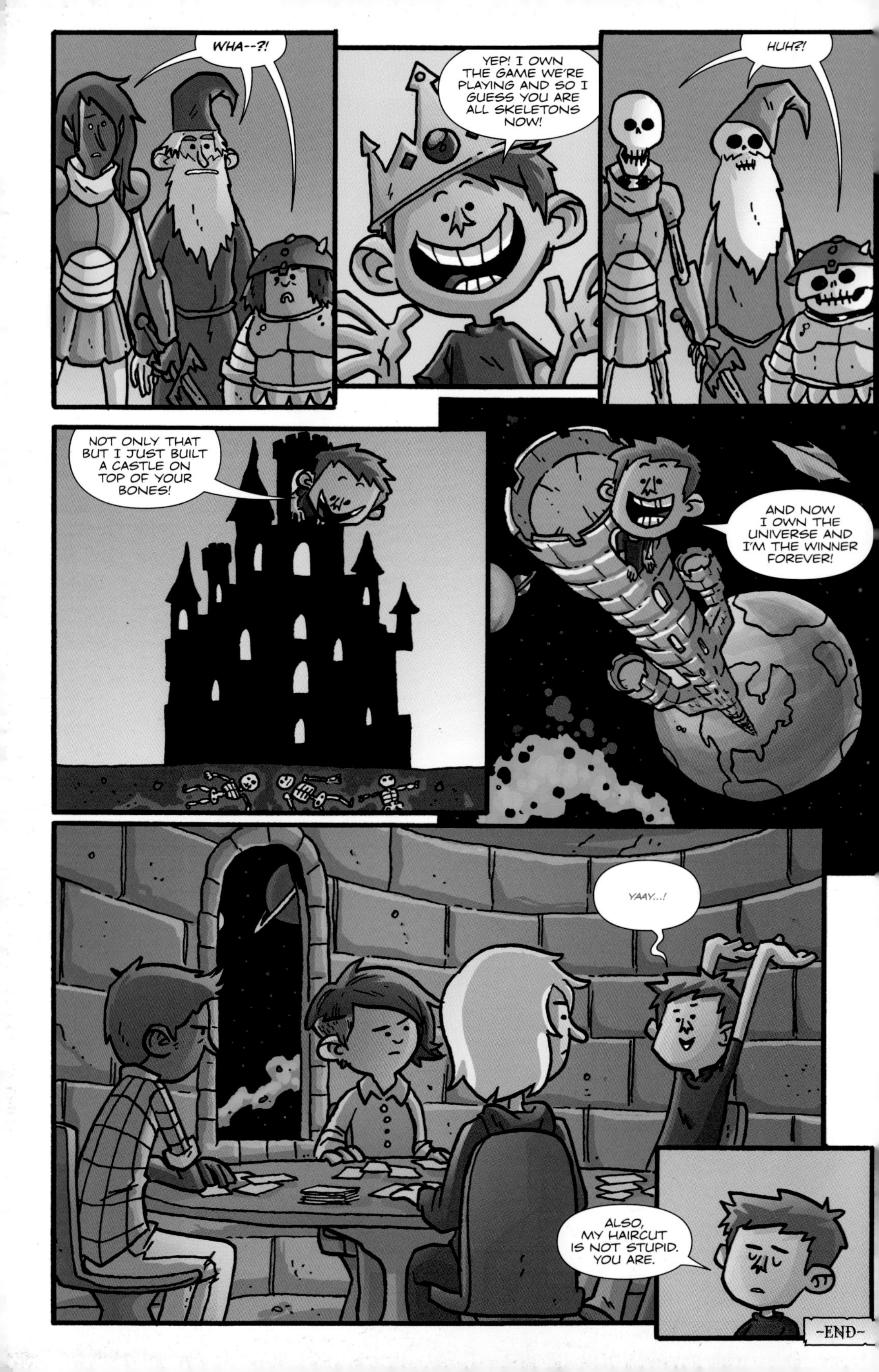
WHA--?!
YEP! I OWN THE GAME WE'RE PLAYING AND SO I GUESS YOU ARE ALL SKELETONS NOW!
HUH?!
NOT ONLY THAT BUT I JUST BUILT A CASTLE ON TOP OF YOUR BONES!
AND NOW I OWN THE UNIVERSE AND I'M THE WINNER FOREVER!
YAAY...!
ALSO, MY HAIRCUT IS NOT STUPID. YOU ARE.
-END-

MUNCHKIN

"READY for Anything"

Written by Jim Zub
Art by Rian Sygh

SOMEWHERE IN A DUNGEON--
DON'T FALL BEHIND!
O-OKAY...
A-HA!
THIS RIGHT **HERE...** THIS IS **EXACTLY** WHAT I'M **TALKIN'** ABOUT!

I DON'T GET IT, SPYKE... IT LOOKS THE EXACT SAME AS THE OTHER HALLWAY.
I KNOW!
IT'S SO GREAT!
10 X 10 GRIDS...
HALLWAYS STRETCHING IN ALL DIRECTIONS...
DARK, DUSTY, WITH THAT EVER-SLIGHT STENCH OF GOBLIN POOP WAFTING PAST YOUR NOSTRILS...
IT'S THE PERFECT DUNGEON!
MWAHAHAHAHAHAHAHA!
I GET THE VAGUE IMPRESSION YOU'RE NOT AS IMPRESSED BY THIS AS I AM, DIC.
"VIC."
MY NAME'S "VIC."
BOOP
I MEAN, SURE, IT'S AN IMPRESSIVE AMOUNT OF ENGINEERING...
ALL THESE TUNNELS AND STAIRS AND ROOMS AND WHATEVER... BUT WHY'S IT HERE? WHAT'S THE POINT?
OH, GREAT, YOU'RE ONE OF THOSE... THE ONES WHO NEED A "MISSION."

POKE
POKE POKE
I DON'T KNOW WHAT YOU'RE DOING, BUT I'M HERE FOR THREE THINGS...
AD-VEN-TURE!
"ADVENTURE" IS WHAT I DO... AND I'M KITTED OUT FROM HEAD TO TOE!
HORNY HELMET: CLASSIC HEADGEAR WITH FINELY POLISHED HORN-AMENTATION!
WARSCREWDRIVER: 18% MORE USEFUL THAN A WARHAMMER.
SNEAKY BASTARD SWORD: STEALTH AND POWER, ALL IN ONE.
BOOTS OF BUTT-KICKING: SELF EXPLANATORY.
TORCH: GOOD FOR SEEING WHERE YOU'RE GOING, UNTIL THE STICK RUNS OUT.
RAT ON A STICK: HEY, IT'S BETTER THAN NOTHING!
YOU'RE CLEARLY NEW HERE.
I DON'T HAVE MUCH XP, BUT I'M TRYING...
"TRY" RHYMES WITH "DIE!"
YOU CAN'T JUST "TRY", RIC, YOU'VE GOTTA "CONQUER!"
UM... WHAT'S "CONQUER" RHYME WITH?

WE TURN A CORNER AND WHO KNOWS WHAT HORRIFIC DANGER LIES AHEAD...
A LIZARD GUY
CENTAUR
GAZEBO
MAYBE EVEN THE KOALA OF CTHULHU!
IF YOU'RE NOT READY FOR BATTLE, THEN THAT'S IT--
GAME OVER!
SURE, BUT--
AND IT'S NOT JUST THE BEASTIES THAT'LL GETCHA, NIC! NO-NO!
CRACK

LOTS O' BURNING
THIS WHOLE PLACE IS CURSED WITH TRICKS AND TRAPS!
DARTS, SCYTHING BLADES, AND BURNING PITS OF HELLFIRE!
AAH!
EVERY STEP COULD BE YOUR LAST!
THUNK
HOLY COW'S MILK!
I HAD NO IDEA IT WAS THIS BAD!
IT'S A GOOD THING WE'RE WORKING TOGETHER...
OH, BUT THAT'S JUST IT, SLIC...
THERE ARE NO TEAMS, ONLY TEMPORARY ALLIANCES.
Huh?
Scoot
SHOVE
DOWN HERE IT'S EVERY MUNCHKIN FOR THEMSELVES...
Eep?

AH!
GHHHHHHHHH
FOOSH
SIGH
THEM'S THE **BREAKS,** KID.
AFTER ALL THIS TIME ON THE QUESTING CIRCUIT, IF THERE'S **ONE** THING I'VE LEARNED DOWN HERE...
Heh, heh, heh...
...IT'S THAT YOU'VE GOTTA BE ***READY FOR ANYTHING.***
END

DEATH FROM BELOW
PLAYTROLL
PLAYTROLL

CHAPTER TWO

MIGHT MAKES WIGHT
PART 1
The Puff of Smoke
WAKE UP, SPYKE!
IT'S TIME FOR ADVENTURE!

HEH, YOU THINK I'M JUST SLEEPING, FLOWER?
BUT...
I AM READY!
YOU THINK I'M JUST HERE TO WAKE YOU UP?
BUT I'M READY TOO!
BUT YOU SHOULD STILL HURRY UP. BREAKFAST BUFFET ENDS AT SEVEN.
RELAX, THIS IS A SIXTEEN PAGE COMIC. ENOUGH TIME FOR BREAKFAST AT THE BEGINNING, A MIDDLE, AND MAYBE A TWIST ENDING!

SO, YOU ARE SET TO RETURN TO THE WIGHT BROTHERS' DUNGEON?
RECEPTION

YOU DO NOT KNOW THE **DANGERS** YOU FACE. THE DUNGEON CONSUMES ALL WHO VENTURE INTO ITS DEPTHS.

CONSUMES NUTHIN'! WE GO ADVENTURING FOR LOOT! LAST TIME WE GOT THIS **SINGING SWORD!**

WE EVEN GOT THIS **SINGING AND DANCING SWORD!**

AND THIS SINGING, DANCING AND **ACTING** SWORD!
There's a fine line between the Method actor and the schizophrenic...

FOOLS! THE WIGHT BROTHERS LURE YOU WITH MATERIAL WEALTH!

SMALL COMFORTS WHEN YOUR LIVES ARE IN THEIR BONY GRASP!

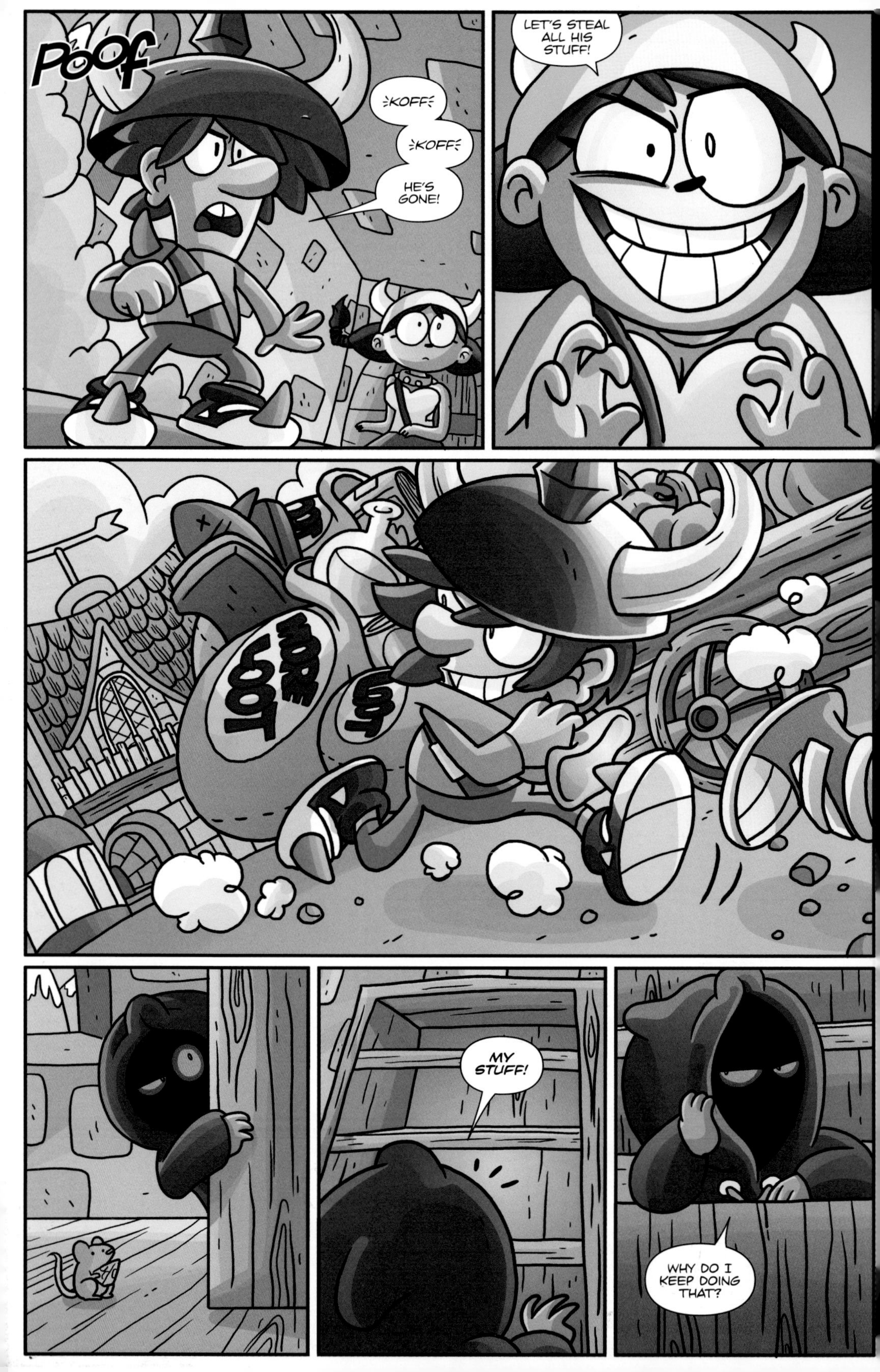
POOF
KOFF
KOFF
HE'S GONE!
LET'S STEAL ALL HIS STUFF!
MORE LOOT
LOOT
MY STUFF!
WHY DO I KEEP DOING THAT?

LOOT
LOOT
MORE LOOT
LOOT

LOOT
LOOT
LOOT

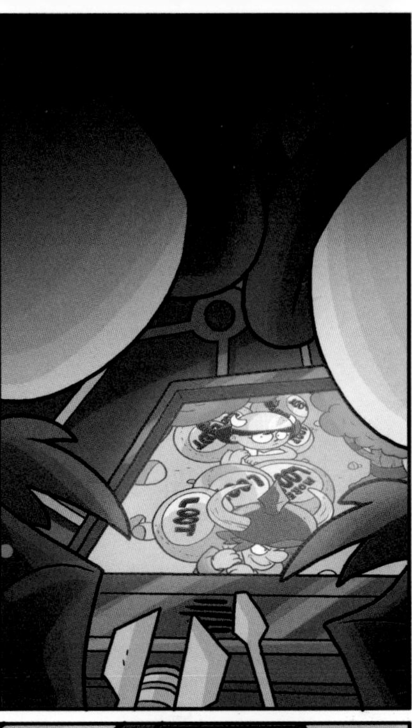

YESSSSS.
MORE FLESSHHH FOR THE GRINDERRR...

Wight Brothers'
ADVENTURE DUNGEON
and shoe repair
LOOT
LOOT

MORE FLESH FOR THE GRINDER!
LOOT

AND BY FLESH I MEAN LOOT.
AND BY GRINDER I MEAN US.
MORE LOOT FOR THE US.

TEAM TALK!
TEAM TALK
TREASURE = good MONSTERS = BAD
OKAY, WE SHOWED SOME GOOD HUSTLE YESTERDAY. I'VE GOT SOME IDEAS FOR TODAY'S GAME PLAN.
SOUNDS GOOD, SOUNDS GOOD.

HARPIES!

LET ME SEE THE GAME PLAN AGAIN.

GOT IT!

DEFEATING HARPIES IS EASY. YOU JUST BREAK THEIR NECKS!
SPYKE! PRETTY HARSH!
YOU SEE, THIS PART IS THE NECK OF THE HARP.
CRACK
MY GRANDFATHER GAVE ME THAT HARP...
WELL, YOU KNOW WHAT THEY SAY ABOUT A HARPLESS HARPY.
WHAT'S THAT?
THEY SAY...
SHUT UP AND GET LOST.

BOOT
THIS STINKS! IT'S BIGFOOT!

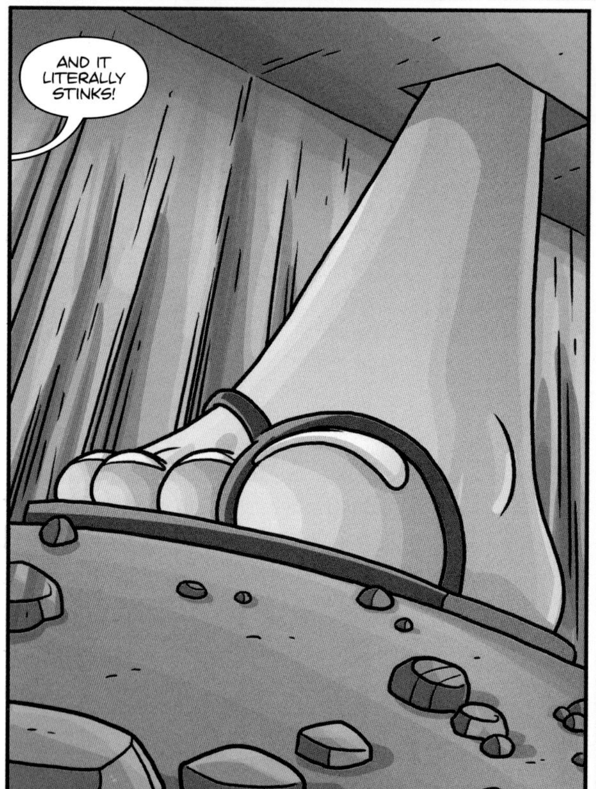
AND IT LITERALLY STINKS!

BUT YOU KNOW BIGFOOT IS JUST A MYTH RIGHT? THEY PROVED IT'S FALSE.
OH YEAH, I READ THAT ARTICLE TOO.

SORRY ABOUT THAT!
SEE YA!

BYE!

RUMMMBLE
THIS COULD BE A PROBLEM...

MAYBE NOT...

I JUST FOUND A CHAINMAIL BIKINI!

YES! I CAN USE THIS!

BOOM
BOY, THAT BIKINI SURE WAS DYNAMITE!
AND LOOK! WE BROKE THROUGH TO THE NEXT ROOM!
WAIT, WAIT.
THIS FEELS WRONG... BREAKING THROUGH THE DUNGEON WALLS FEEL LIKE CHEATING...
AND WHO SAYS WE CAN'T CHEAT? IT'S NOT LIKE THERE'S A SIGN THAT SAYS *NO CHEATING!*
WELL, EXCEPT FOR THIS SIGN RIGHT HERE.
NO CHEATING

ACID PIT

WHAT SIGN?

WELL, IF YOU PUT IT THAT WAY...
LET'S GO!
BAT!
BRRMMMM
BRMMMMM
ORC-B-GONE
tink
tink

DUNGEON CASINO
YES! DOUBLE SEVENS!
WELCOME TO STAR MUNCHKIN, GENTS!
HERE'S YOUR CARDS!
YOU LOSE!
OOH! TOUGH LUCK! THIS IS A LOSING HAND.
WHICH MEANS YOU HAVE TO GIVE ME ALL YOUR STUFF.
HAHAHAHA!

SCREEECH!
GRRAARHH!

I DON'T THINK WE CAN USE CARD TRICKS AGAINST THIS GUY...
LET'S TRY THIS BOTTLE OF POLYMORPH POTION INSTEAD!
CRASH
ZOOP!
HAHAHA! NICE!
FWOOOOSH
WAAAAH!
OKAY, SO THAT DIDN'T WORK! YOU GOT ANY IDEAS?

WELL, MAKING HIM SMALLER DIDN'T WORK...
HUMONGOUS POTION
LET'S MAKE HIM BIGGER!
LOB!
WHAA?
BLOOOP
CRASH
RAWWWK!
bwoooOOSh

CC
TV

BROTHER. THESE TWO ARE DESTROYING OUR DUNGEON.

I AGREE, BROTHER.
BUT THIS IS ALL ACCORDING TO THE PLAN.
CC
TV

HIS PLANS ARE BEYOND OUR MEAGER GRASP, ALL WE CAN HOPE IS TO FOLLOW THEM...

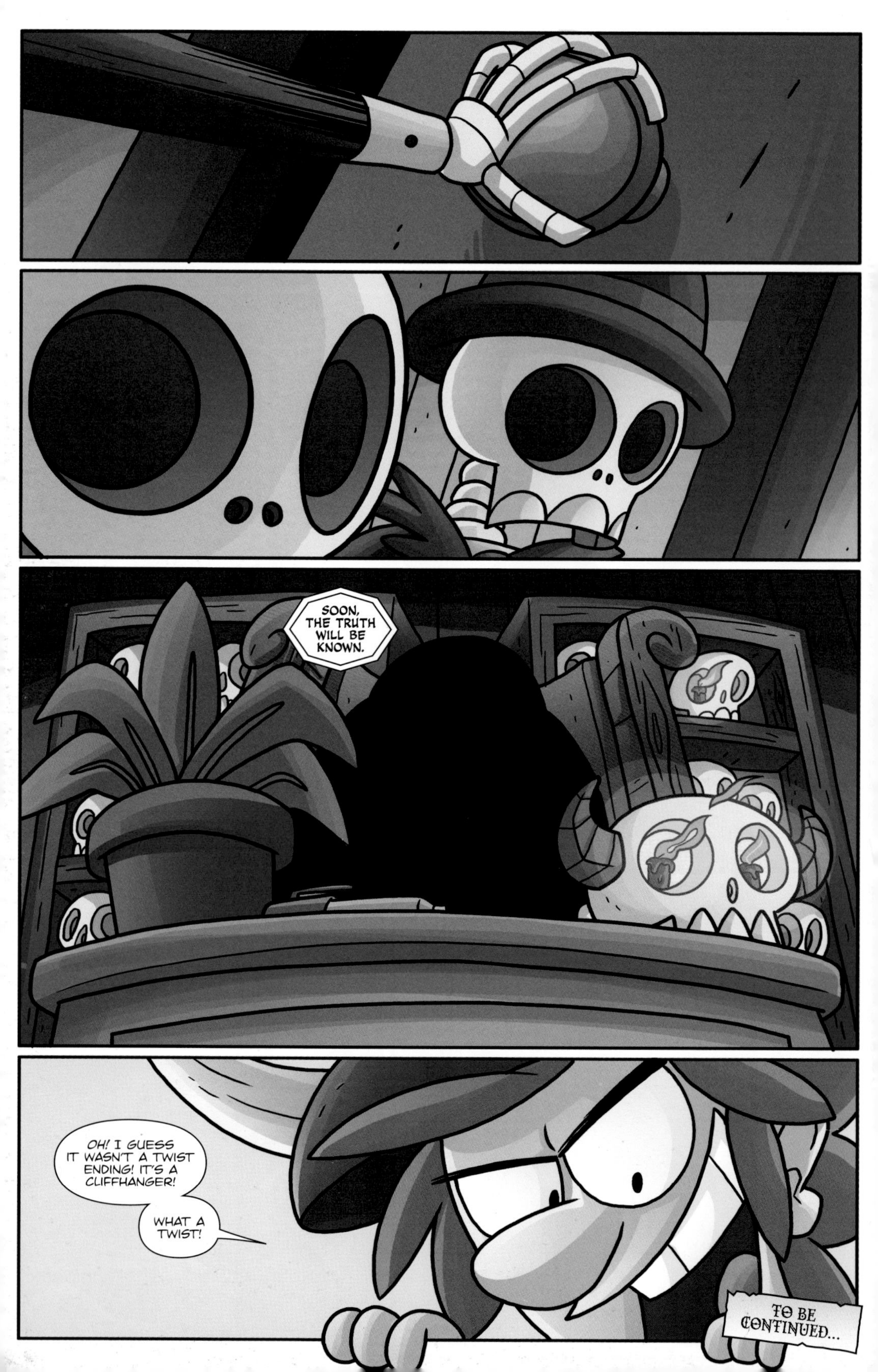
SOON, THE TRUTH WILL BE KNOWN.
OH! I GUESS IT WASN'T A TWIST ENDING! IT'S A CLIFFHANGER!
WHAT A TWIST!
TO BE CONTINUED...

Sniff

Sniff

Sniff

Sniff

AS MUNCHKINS GO ABOUT THEIR ENDLESS QUESTS, **SLAYING** MONSTERS BIG AND SMALL, IT'S EASY TO **FORGET** THAT EACH OF THESE **WONDERFULLY UNIQUE CREATURES** HAS THEIR OWN **STORY** TO TELL.

MUNCHKIN

Story by Jim Zub
Art by Rian Sygh

SNORT

Sniff

AND THUS, BELOVED READER, WE'RE PROUD TO PRESENT...

The Ecology of the FLOATING NOSE

FIRST IN A SERIES OF MEMES *(Munchkin Education Monsters Essays).*

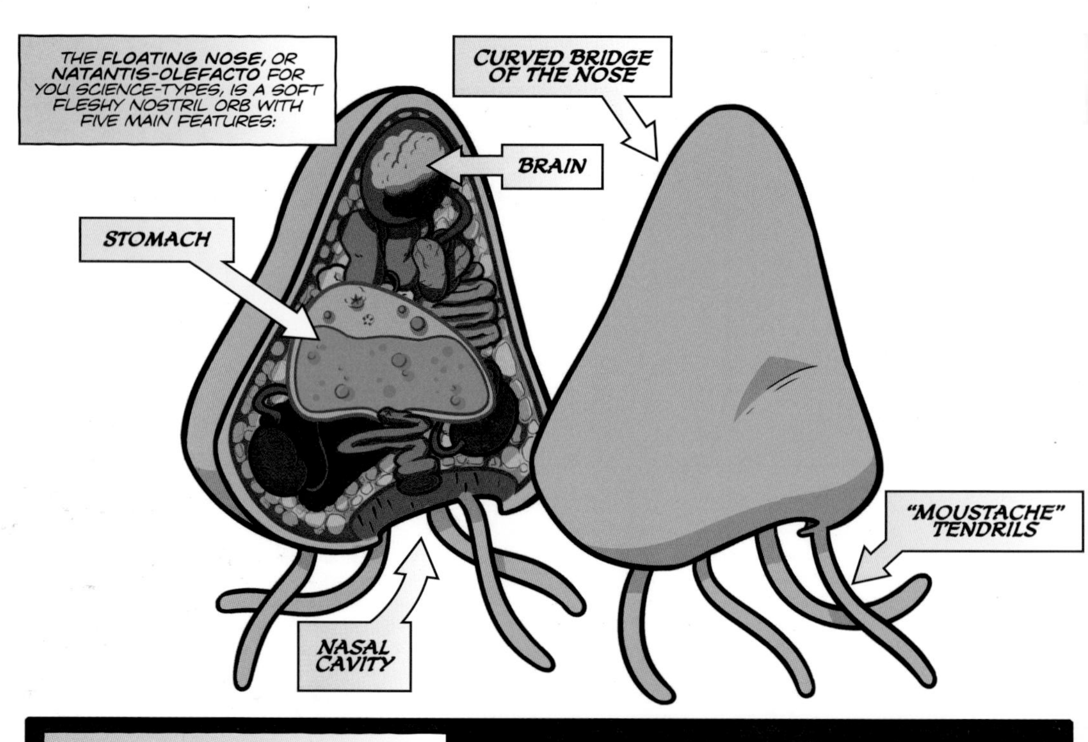
THE FLOATING NOSE, OR NATANTIS-OLEFACTO FOR YOU SCIENCE-TYPES, IS A SOFT FLESHY NOSTRIL ORB WITH FIVE MAIN FEATURES:
CURVED BRIDGE OF THE NOSE
BRAIN
STOMACH
"MOUSTACHE" TENDRILS
NASAL CAVITY

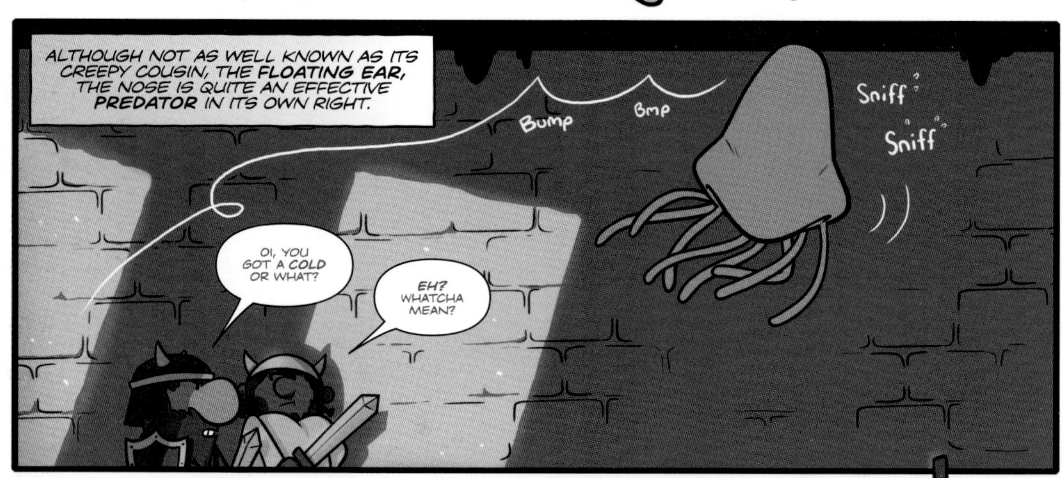
ALTHOUGH NOT AS WELL KNOWN AS ITS CREEPY COUSIN, THE FLOATING EAR, THE NOSE IS QUITE AN EFFECTIVE PREDATOR IN ITS OWN RIGHT.
Bump
Bmp
Sniff
Sniff
OI, YOU GOT A COLD OR WHAT?
EH? WHATCHA MEAN?

WE'RE S'POSED TA BE SNEAKIN', BUT YU KEEP SNIFFLIN'!
Sniff
BLOW YER HOSE OR I'LL CUT IT OFF!
T'AIN'T ME! I THOUGHT IT WAS YU!

SNIFF!
AAAHH

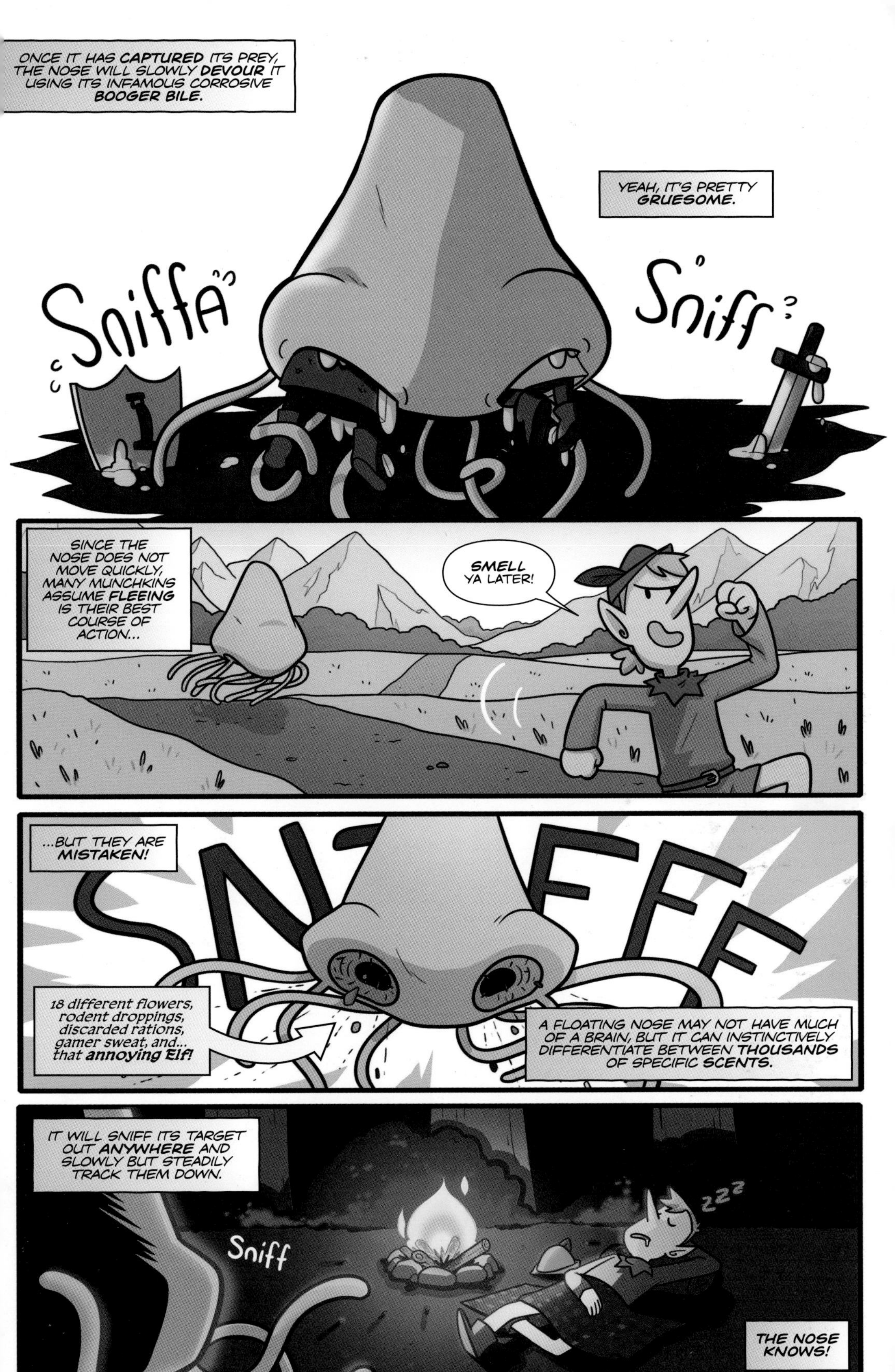
ONCE IT HAS CAPTURED ITS PREY, THE NOSE WILL SLOWLY DEVOUR IT USING ITS INFAMOUS CORROSIVE BOOGER BILE.
YEAH, IT'S PRETTY GRUESOME.
SNIFFA
SNIFF
SINCE THE NOSE DOES NOT MOVE QUICKLY, MANY MUNCHKINS ASSUME FLEEING IS THEIR BEST COURSE OF ACTION...
SMELL YA LATER!
...BUT THEY ARE MISTAKEN!
18 different flowers, rodent droppings, discarded rations, gamer sweat, and... that annoying Elf!
A FLOATING NOSE MAY NOT HAVE MUCH OF A BRAIN, BUT IT CAN INSTINCTIVELY DIFFERENTIATE BETWEEN THOUSANDS OF SPECIFIC SCENTS.
IT WILL SNIFF ITS TARGET OUT ANYWHERE AND SLOWLY BUT STEADILY TRACK THEM DOWN.
SNIFF
ZZZ
THE NOSE KNOWS!

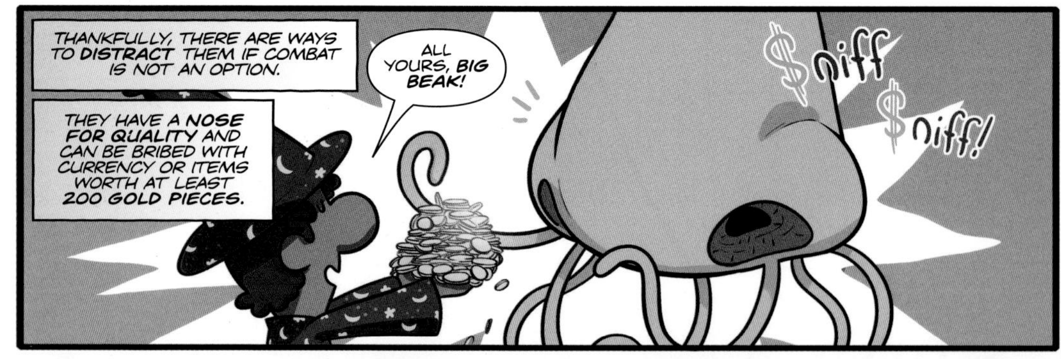

THANKFULLY, THERE ARE WAYS TO DISTRACT THEM IF COMBAT IS NOT AN OPTION.
THEY HAVE A NOSE FOR QUALITY AND CAN BE BRIBED WITH CURRENCY OR ITEMS WORTH AT LEAST 200 GOLD PIECES.
ALL YOURS, BIG BEAK!
$niff
$niff!

THAT MOOLAH IS USED AS PART OF THE NOSEY COURTING CEREMONY.
Sn♡ff
Sn♡ff!

AFTER A 9 MONTH NASAL CONGESTION, 2-4 LITTLE BOOGERS ARE EXCAVATED AND JOIN THE FAMILY.
Sni
Sni
Sni
Sni
Sni
Sniff
Sniff

FLOATING NOSES GROW RELATIVELY QUICKLY, DEPENDING ON THEIR OLFACTORY UPBRINGING, AND REACH FULL SNORT WITHIN A YEAR OR TWO.

CHILD
Button Nose

TEEN
Nose It All

ADULT
Standard Snout

ELDERLY
Ye Olde Schnozzle

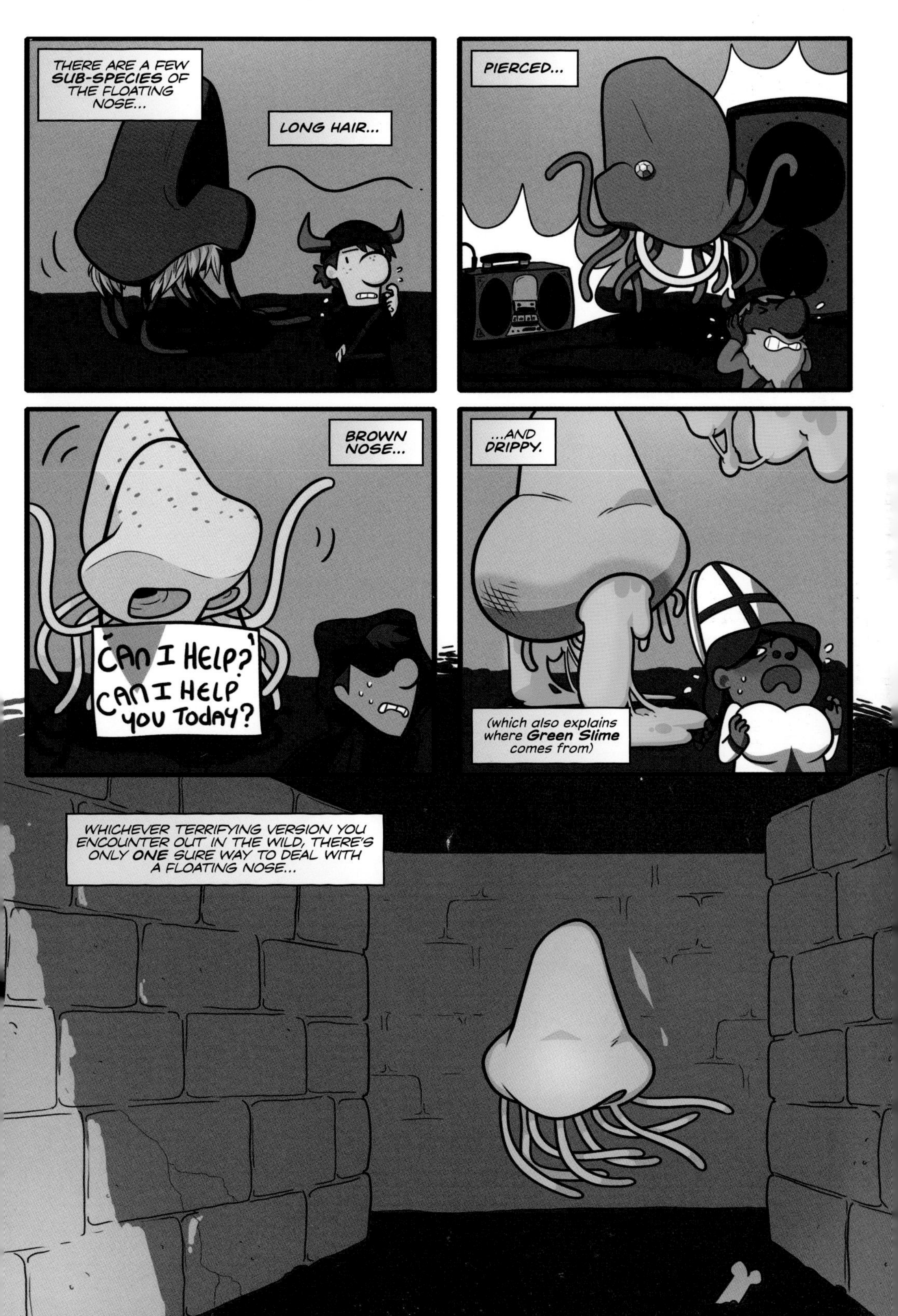
THERE ARE A FEW SUB-SPECIES OF THE FLOATING NOSE...
LONG HAIR...
PIERCED...
BROWN NOSE...
CAN I HELP? CAN I HELP YOU TODAY?
...AND DRIPPY.
(which also explains where Green Slime comes from)
WHICHEVER TERRIFYING VERSION YOU ENCOUNTER OUT IN THE WILD, THERE'S ONLY ONE SURE WAY TO DEAL WITH A FLOATING NOSE...

Sniff!
Sniffles
Extra Soft
IT SNOT GOING TO WORK!
THIS BLOWS!
Sniff!

SLAIN FLOATING NOSES ARE USUALLY DISPLAYED AS TROPHIES...
THESE "STUFFED" NOSES CAN BE QUITE A STATUS SYMBOL AMONGST MUNCHKIN VETERANS.
WHADDAYA CALL A GIANT NOSE FLOATING AROUND WITHOUT A BODY?!
HMMM...
NOBODY NOSE!
GROAN
NO SPELLCASTING OR LOOTING (BRAWLING OK)
SO, UNTIL NEXT TIME, KEEP YOUR NOSE OUT OF OTHER PEOPLE'S BUSINESS.
-END-

DEATH FROM BELOW
PLAYTROLL
PLAYTROLL

CHAPTER THREE

SPYKE
FLOWER
PREVIOUSLY, ON MUNCHKIN.
INTREPID ADVENTURERS SPYKE AND FLOWER PLUNGED INTO THE DEPTHS OF THE WIGHT BROTHERS' DUNGEON...
SPYKE
FLOWER
WHERE THEY BESTED THE OBSTACLES BEFORE THEM AND LAID WASTE TO THE PERILOUS LABYRINTH.
LITTLE DO THEY KNOW... THE WIGHT BROTHERS WATCH THEIR EVERY MOVE...
ARE SPYKE AND FLOWER HEADING FOR A DEADLY TRAP?
THE ANSWER IS YES, IN...

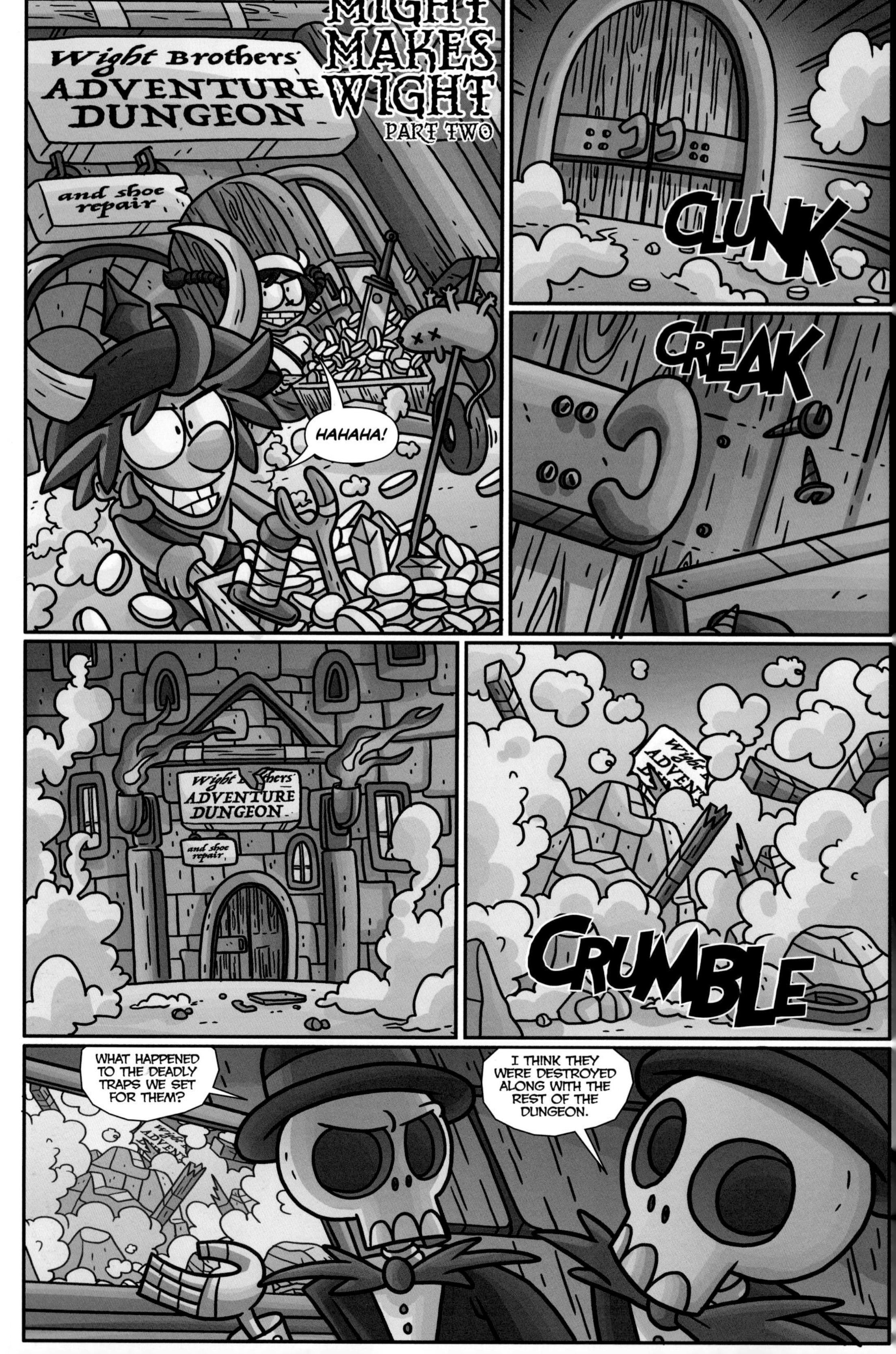
MIGHT MAKES WIGHT
PART TWO
Wight Brothers ADVENTURE DUNGEON
and shoe repair
HAHAHA!
CLUNK
CREAK
Wight Brothers ADVENTURE DUNGEON
and shoe repair
CRUMBLE
WHAT HAPPENED TO THE DEADLY TRAPS WE SET FOR THEM?
I THINK THEY WERE DESTROYED ALONG WITH THE REST OF THE DUNGEON.

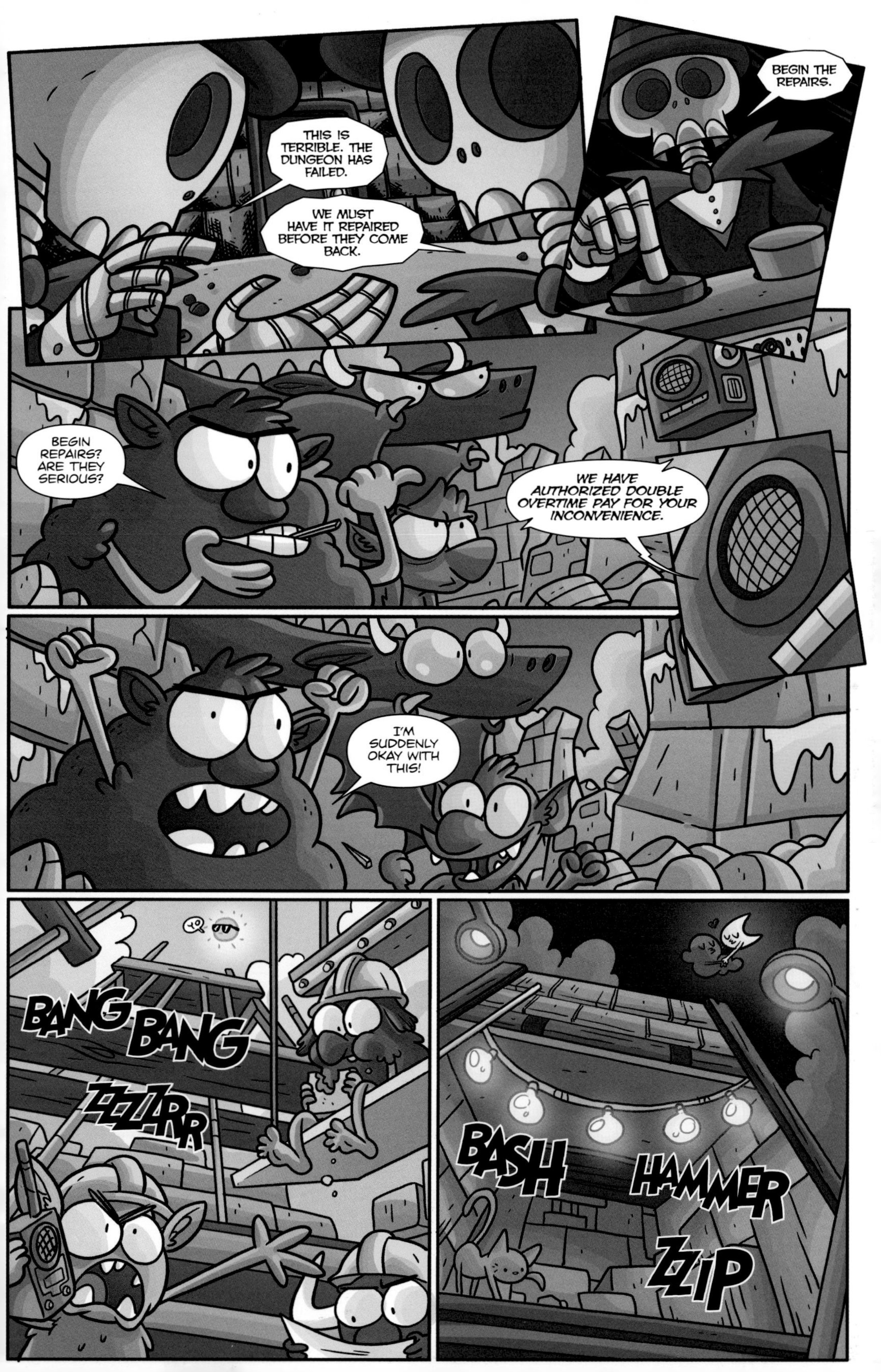
THIS IS TERRIBLE. THE DUNGEON HAS FAILED.
WE MUST HAVE IT REPAIRED BEFORE THEY COME BACK.
BEGIN THE REPAIRS.
BEGIN REPAIRS? ARE THEY SERIOUS?
WE HAVE AUTHORIZED DOUBLE OVERTIME PAY FOR YOUR INCONVENIENCE.
I'M SUDDENLY OKAY WITH THIS!
YO
BANG BANG
ZZZARR
BASH
HAMMER
ZZIP

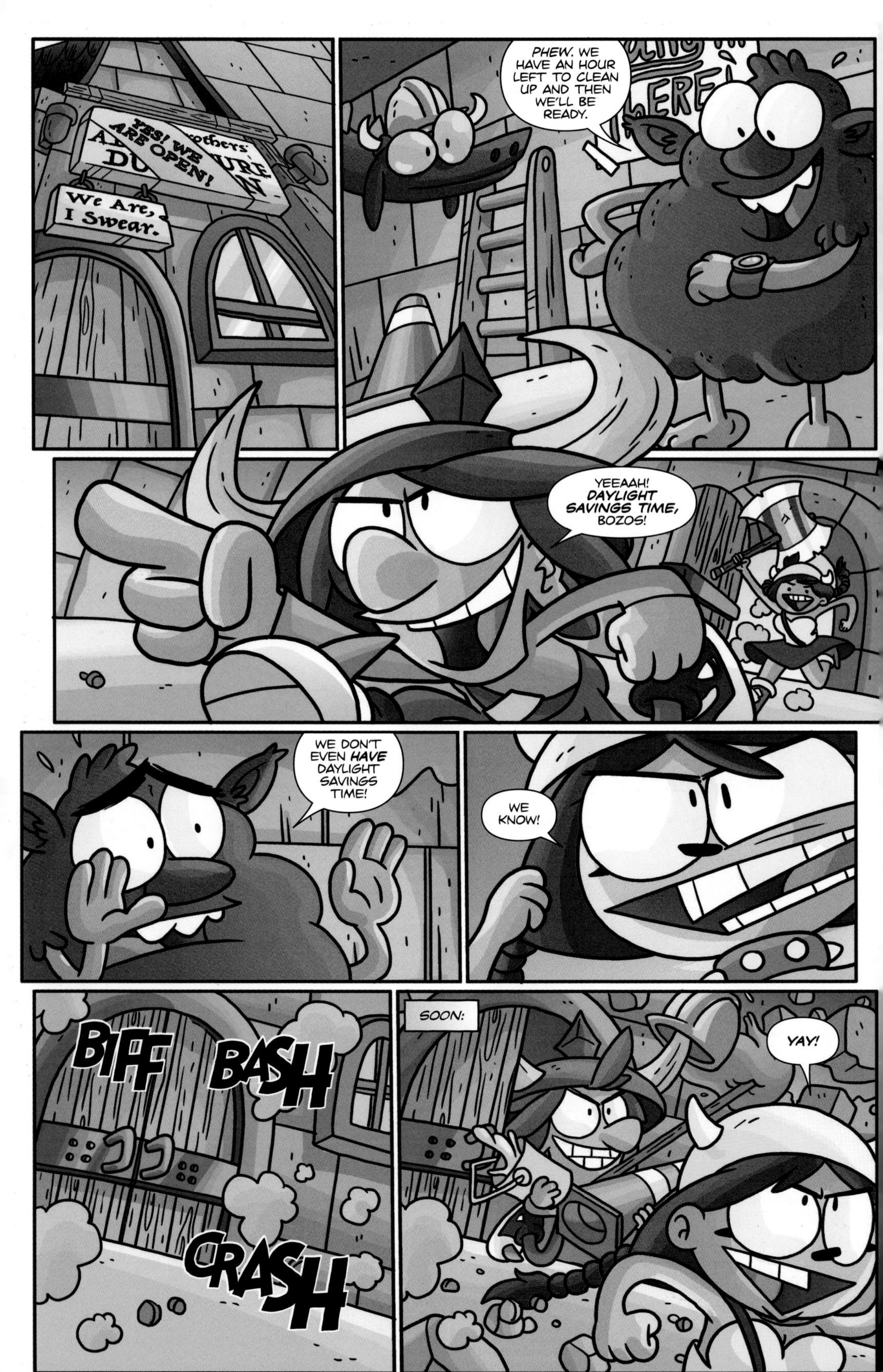

YES! WE ARE OPEN!
We Are, I Swear.
PHEW. WE HAVE AN HOUR LEFT TO CLEAN UP AND THEN WE'LL BE READY.
YEEAAH! ***DAYLIGHT SAVINGS TIME,*** BOZOS!
WE DON'T EVEN ***HAVE*** DAYLIGHT SAVINGS TIME!
WE KNOW!
BIFF
BASH
CRASH
SOON:
YAY!

UH...WE AUTHORIZE TRIPLE OVERTIME TO REBUILD THE DUNGEON...
UGGGHHHH...
UNDER CONSTRUCTION
AGAIN
Wight Brothers' ADVENTURE DUNGEON
RE-RE-OPENING
WET PAINT
YEAH! BRITISH SUMMERTIME!
CRASH

OKAY, QUADRUPLE OVERTIME FO--
ZZZKKK
CRUNCH

NOW, DID WE START TO FEEL BAD FOR THOSE DUNGEON GUYS AT THIS POINT? OF COURSE WE DID. OF COURSE.
BUT YOU HAVE TO UNDERSTAND.

YOU SEE, INSIDE THE DUNGEON IS STUFF. AND, WELL, WE WANT THAT STUFF.
AND TO HAVE THAT STUFF, WE HAVE TO TAKE IT. FROM THEM. IN THE DUNGEON.

BECAUSE HAVING MATERIAL POSSESSIONS MAKES US HAPPY.
THAT'S WHAT WE DECIDED, YEAH.

THE WIGHT BROTHERS, MAN, THEY HAD NO IDEA WHAT IT WAS LIKE.
"REBUILD THE DUNGEON" "REBUILD THE DUNGEON" YAK YAK YAK!
AS IF THROWING MONEY AT THE PROBLEM WILL MAKE IT GO AWAY.
BUT LET ME TELL YOU. BY THE END OF THE WEEK, THERE WAS NO MONEY. THERE WERE NO MATERIALS. THERE WASN'T EVEN ANYTHING LEFT TO REBUILD!

I HOPE THEY HAVE MORE TINS OF PAINT. THE LAST HAUL WAS SO GOOD!
OH! OR TUBS OF SPACKLE!
I JUST CAN'T GET OVER HOW COOL THIS NEW RAT ON A STICK IS!
HUH.
SPROING
AHA! FIRST MONSTER OF THE DAY!
!
crumple

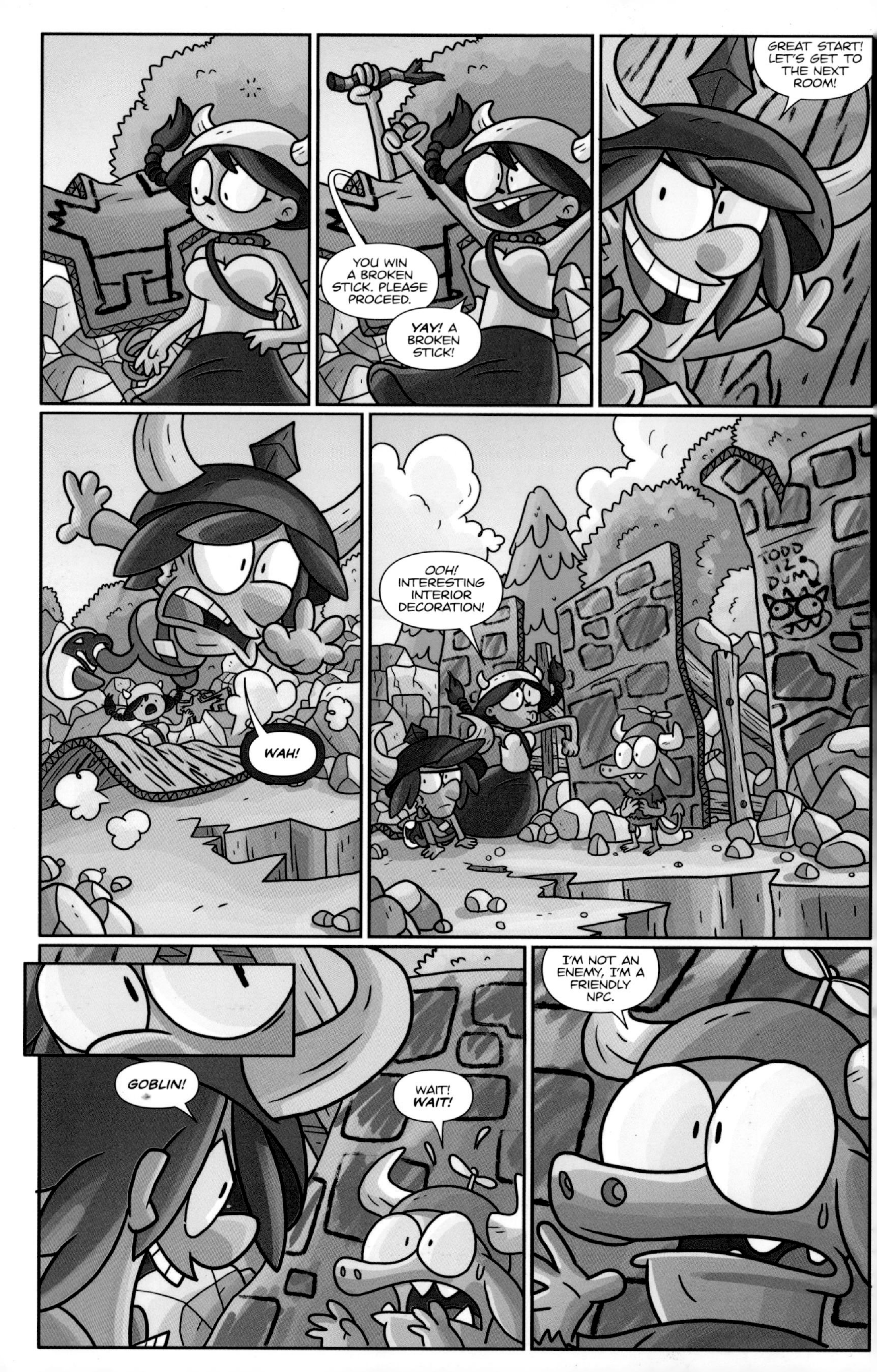

YOU WIN A BROKEN STICK. PLEASE PROCEED.
YAY! A BROKEN STICK!
GREAT START! LET'S GET TO THE NEXT ROOM!
WAH!
OOH! INTERESTING INTERIOR DECORATION!
TODD IZ DUM
GOBLIN!
WAIT! WAIT!
I'M NOT AN ENEMY, I'M A FRIENDLY NPC.

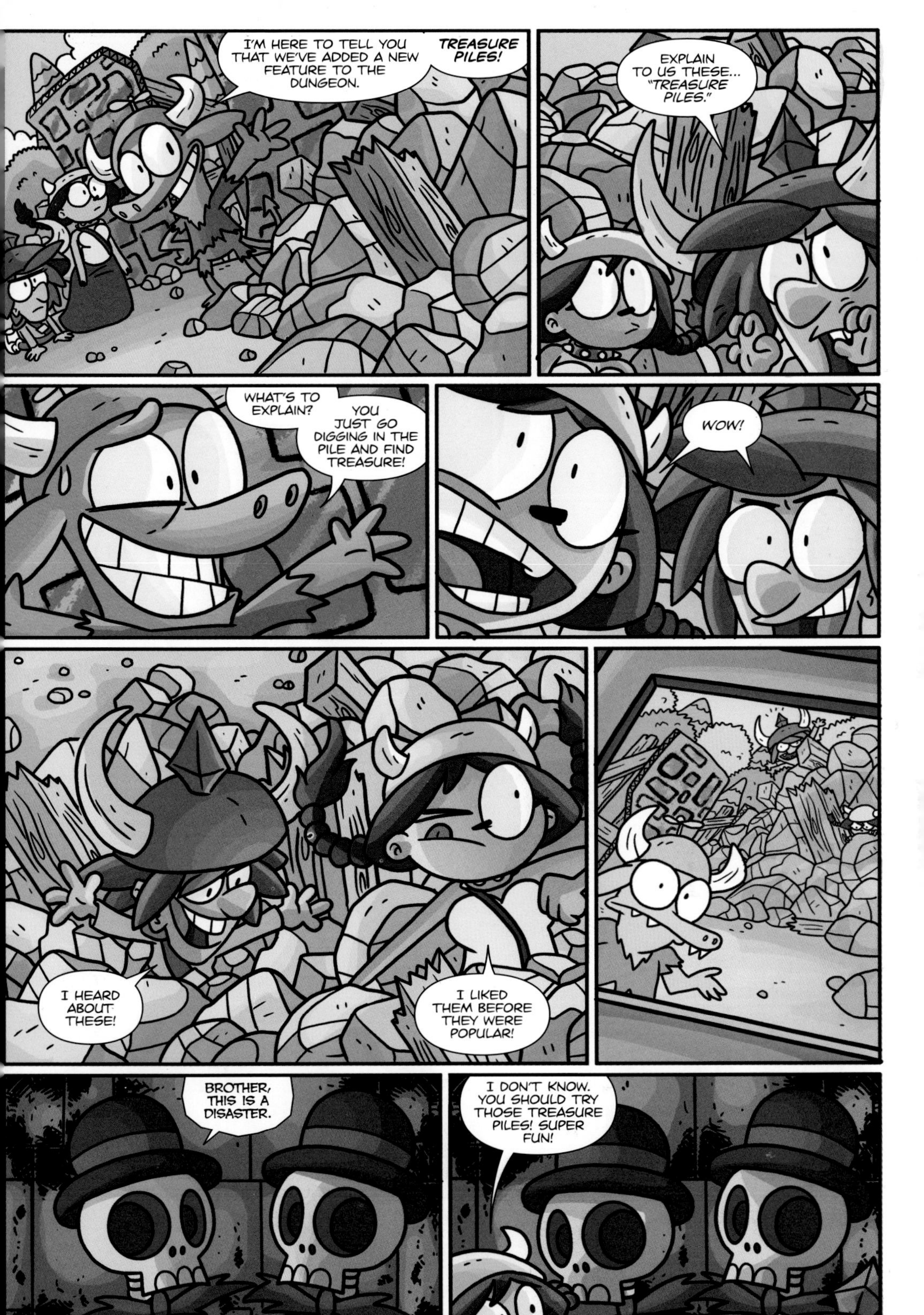
I'M HERE TO TELL YOU THAT WE'VE ADDED A NEW FEATURE TO THE DUNGEON.
TREASURE PILES!
EXPLAIN TO US THESE... "TREASURE PILES."
WHAT'S TO EXPLAIN?
YOU JUST GO DIGGING IN THE PILE AND FIND TREASURE!
WOW!
I HEARD ABOUT THESE!
I LIKED THEM BEFORE THEY WERE POPULAR!
BROTHER, THIS IS A DISASTER.
YES. THIS IS BARELY A DUNGEON AT ALL. THE BOSS WILL BE DISPLEASED.
I DON'T KNOW. YOU SHOULD TRY THOSE TREASURE PILES! SUPER FUN!

YOU! HOW DID YOU GET IN HERE?!
OH, I FOUND THIS KEY IN A TREASURE PILE! IT LET ME OPEN A DOOR THAT SAID SOMETHING ABOUT "AUTHORIZED ACCESS" OR WHATEVER.
YEAH, AND IT LED TO THIS SMALL ROOM WITH A MONSTER INSIDE, SO WE DEFEATED IT, AND THEN FOUND THIS ROOM HERE!

SMALL ROOM WITH A MONSTER...
THAT WAS OUR ADMINISTRATION OFFICE!
hang in there!

BUT...IF YOU ARE HERE, WHY CAN WE STILL SEE YOU ON OUR DUNGEON MONITORS?!

I DON'T KNOW. BROADCAST DELAY? YOU REALLY NEED TO UPDATE YOUR EQUIPMENT.
IS MY NOSE REALLY THAT BIG?

THE BOSS WILL BE VERY DISPLEASED.

THAT'S THE SECOND TIME YOU MENTIONED A BOSS! WHERE IS HE?!
A BOSS? YOU MEAN LIKE A FINAL BOSS OF THE DUNGEON?
WHERE?! WHERE?!
BOSS
IS HE IN HERE?!
YE--NO! HE'S NOT!
BOSS
HMMM...
WAIT! I THINK IT'S A TRICK! THERE ARE NO OTHER DOORS AND THIS ONE SAYS "BOSS" ON IT.
HMMMMM...
HA! YOU GUYS! YOU ALMOST HAD US!

VERY WELL. ON YOUR HEAD BE IT.
CREAK
BOSS

PRETTY DARK IN HERE GUYS.

FOUND THE LIGHTS!

NO! THE BOSS *HATES* LIGHT!

UH... WHAT BOSS?
THIS IS OUR BOSS, HERE.
THIS IS YOUR BOSS.
YES.
THIS POTTED PLANT, RIGHT HERE.
IS YOUR BOSS.
YES.
YES.
YOU UNDERSTAND THAT PLANTS *LIKE* AND *REQUIRE* LIGHT, DON'T YOU?
THEY DO?!
WHY IS YOUR BOSS A POTTED PLANT?!

WE FOUND THE BOSS DURING OUR TRAVELS.
WHEN WE SAW HIM, WE COULD DO NOTHING BUT BOW DOWN TO HIS SUPERIORITY.
HE WHISPERED TO US. IN A VOICE ONLY WE COULD HEAR.
A VOICE THAT PULSED IN HIS LEAVES AND VIBRATED THROUGH HIS VEINS. A CODED SONG, SINGING OUT FOR DEATH AND DESTRUCTION.

I SEE.
AND... DO PLANTS OFTEN SING TO YOU ABOUT DEATH AND DESTRUCTION?
WELL, YES.
PRETTY MUCH EVERYTHING SOUNDS LIKE A SONG OF DEATH TO US.
WE ARE WIGHTS AFTER ALL.
ONE TIME MY BROTHER CHANGED HIS RINGTONE TO ***HOLLABACK GIRL*** AND I STARTED DIGGING PIT TRAPS EVERY TIME HE GOT A CALL.
CRASH

NOOO!
BOSS!
WE FOUND SOMETHING ELSE IN THE ADMIN OFFICE.
WE FOUND THE DEEDS TO THE ENTIRE DUNGEON.
AND WE ALSO FOUND FINANCIAL REPORTS THAT SAY YOU'VE BEEN PAYING YOUR WORKERS... QUADRUPLE OVERTIME?
OH MY, AND BILLS FOR BUILDING MATERIALS AND EXTRAS?
BASICALLY, GENTLEMEN, YOU ARE BROKE.
AND SINCE WE WON ALL YOUR MONEY AND "DEFEATED" YOUR BOSS...

IT LOOKS LIKE YOU WORK FOR US NOW!
AND WE CAN SET UP THE NEXT DUNGEON HOWEVER WE WANT!
-THE END-

BEYOND THE REASONABLE "EAT YOUR VEGGIES AND GET A GOOD NIGHT'S SLEEP" EDGE OF **SANITY,** THERE LIE A WHOLE BUNCH OF **SANITY-SMASHING THINGS** YOU **SHOULDN'T** GO LOOKING FOR.

WAIT! DIDN'T YOU **JUST** HEAR ME?!

PUT DOWN THIS COMIC BEFORE IT'S **TOO LATE!**

AW, GEEZ! **NOW** YOU'VE GONE AND **DONE** IT...

THIS IS WHY WE CAN'T HAVE NICE THINGS!

PREPARE YOURSELF FOR THE **UNPREPARABLE!**

NCHKIN

ART BY RIAN SYGH

STORY BY JIM ZUB

MUNCHKIN CTHULHU COMES FOR US ALL!

LURED IN BY THE NARRATOR'S NEED TO GET THIS STORY OF ELDRITCH STUPIDITY UNDERWAY, OUR MUNCHKINS ARE GATHERED TOGETHER TO INVESTIGATE A MYSTERIOUS LOCATION.
THE INVESTIGATOR: LOOKING WHERE SANE PEOPLE OUGHT NOT TO.
I'LL LEAVE NO STONE UNTURNED.
LITERALLY... I'M GONNA ROTATE EVERY ROCK I FIND!
THE PROFESSOR: KNOWLEDGEABLE IN THE LOST ART OF 'BOOK LEARNING'.
DISSERTATION OR BUST, YO.
THE MONSTER WHACKER: HIS GREATEST ASSET IS HIS OBLIVIOUSNESS.
EVERY QUESTION HAS AN ANSWER... AND THAT ANSWER IS "VIOLENCE."
THE CULTIST: 100% LIKELY TO BETRAY THE GROUP FOR HER GIBBERING MASTER FROM BEYOND TIME AND SPACE.
ANYONE WANNA SWIG OF MY ICHOR-LIQUOR?
IT'S R'LYEH GOOD!
YOU'RE ALL DEAD MEAT
OLD AGE HOME
LOOKS LIKE THIS IS THE RIGHT WAY.
HOW DO YOU KNOW?
JUST FOLLOW THE ELDER SIGN...
HEE HEE HEE!
MiSTAH Tonic's "LOVE EM & LEAVE EM" HOME FOR the NEAR DEAD.
M.W., YOU GO FIRST.
I CONCUR. I CALCULATE A HIGH PROBABILITY OF DANGER WITHIN.
I DON'T BELIEVE IN CALCULATORS!

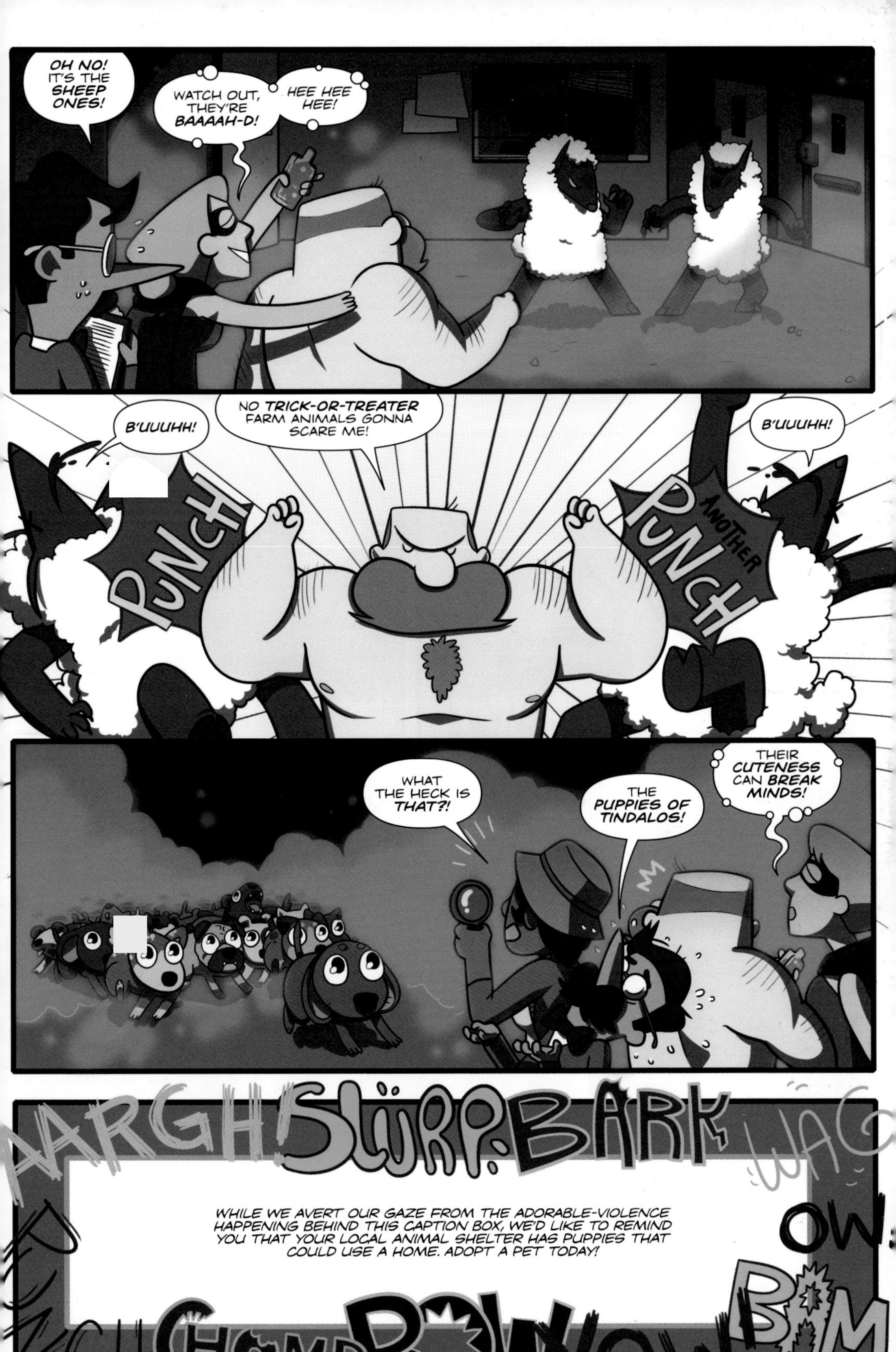
OH NO! IT'S THE SHEEP ONES!
WATCH OUT, THEY'RE BAAAAH-D!
HEE HEE HEE!
B'UUUHH!
NO TRICK-OR-TREATER FARM ANIMALS GONNA SCARE ME!
B'UUUHH!
PUNCH
ANOTHER PUNCH
WHAT THE HECK IS THAT?!
THE PUPPIES OF TINDALOS!
THEIR CUTENESS CAN BREAK MINDS!
AARGH SLURP BARK WAG
WHILE WE AVERT OUR GAZE FROM THE ADORABLE-VIOLENCE HAPPENING BEHIND THIS CAPTION BOX, WE'D LIKE TO REMIND YOU THAT YOUR LOCAL ANIMAL SHELTER HAS PUPPIES THAT COULD USE A HOME. ADOPT A PET TODAY!
OW!
PUNCH CHOMP POW YOW! BAM

WE MADE IT--
THE MASTER CHAMBER!
HEE HEE! IT'S TRUE! THIS IS WHERE MY MASTER HANGS OUT.

LET'S SEE WHAT'S UNDER THESE DUMMY DRAPES!
NOW, LET'S NOT RUSH ANYTHI--

SANITY TREMOR
PULL
--NNG!
THAT'S KINDA WEIRD...

SANITY SHAKE
G'AAH!
SORTA UGLY, AIN'T IT?

SANITY QUAKE
AIEEE!
HMMM... I GIVE IT A 3/10.

SANITY CRUMBLE
DROOOL...
WELL NOW, THAT'S JUST UNFORTUNATE.

DIM-WITTED FOOL, YOU HAVE UNLEASHED THE POWER OF H.P. MUNCHCRAFT!
YOUR VOICE SOUNDS LIKE YOU GARGLE WITH BATTERY ACID, BUD. YOU SHOULD GET THAT CHECKED OUT.
THE TIME IS NIGH!
SERIOUSLY, IT'S NIGH O' CLOCK!
HORRORS UNIMAGINABLE ARRIVE!
GNARLYTHOTEP: SURFER BEYOND THE STARS.
duuuude~
HOG-SOTHOTH: HIS BACON DEVOURS YOUR DREAMS.
oink~
SHRUB-NIGGURATH: HIS POWER IS UNBE-LEAF-ABLE.
rustle~
THT WHCH HS N VWLS: ST_P_D B_T ST_LL D_NG_R__S
BRRRING BRRRING
Dude?
– ph_n_ c_ll?

H_LL_?
HEY!
IT'S ME, THE STEER OF THE DEEP, COWTHULHU!
I'VE GOT A BEEF WITH YOU GUYS...
I MOOED IT VERY CLEAR YOU WERE NOT TO BARBECUE THE UNIVERSE 'TIL I WAS DONE MILKING IT FOR ALL IT'S WORTH!
NO PARTY 'TIL THE COW GOES HOME... GOT IT?!
_K...
Oink...
Duuuude...
rustle, rustle...
HA!
LOOKS LIKE WE SHOWED THOSE COSPLAY-LOSERS WHO'S BOSS, EH GANG?
TWITCH
FOAM
GIBBER
DROOL
UNTIL NEXT TIME, TRY NOT TO STEP IN ANY NON-EUCLIDIAN COW PATTIES.
-END-

DEATH FROM BELOW
PLAYTROLL
PLAYTROLL

CHAPTER FOUR

I THINK WE LOST HER...
HA! IF THE DUNGEON'S TRAPS DON'T GET HER, THE FIRE GLYPHS I LEFT SURELY WILL!

AND WHEN I HAVE NO FURTHER USE FOR YOU, YOU WILL BE NEXT, MY FRIEND...

HUH? WHAT DID YOU SAY?

WHAT? HUH?

SOUNDED LIKE YOU SAID I'LL BE NEXT WHEN YOU HAVE NO USE FOR ME.
HUH? I DIDN'T SAY ANYTHING.
OH, OKAY.

GOOD, I WOULDN'T WANT ANYTHING TO HAPPEN BEFORE YOU MEET YOUR END!

HUH?
WHA?

"BECOME AN ARBORIST," THEY SAID. "ANCIENT LOCKING MECHANISMS IS A USELESS DEGREE," THEY SAID.
WOULD YOU GET ON WITH IT!
GOT IT!

NOT SO FAST, JERKS!

PIX! YOU SURVIVED?!
OOH, AWKWAAARD...
I KNOW TO WEAR MY FIREPROOF BRITCHES BEFORE GOING ANYWHERE WITH YOU, ADAIRE!
SO...YOU'VE DONE THIS KIND OF THING BEFORE?

LOOK, I'M NOT A COMPLICATED PERSON. WE KNOW THERE IS ONLY ONE RULE HERE IN THE DUNGEON...

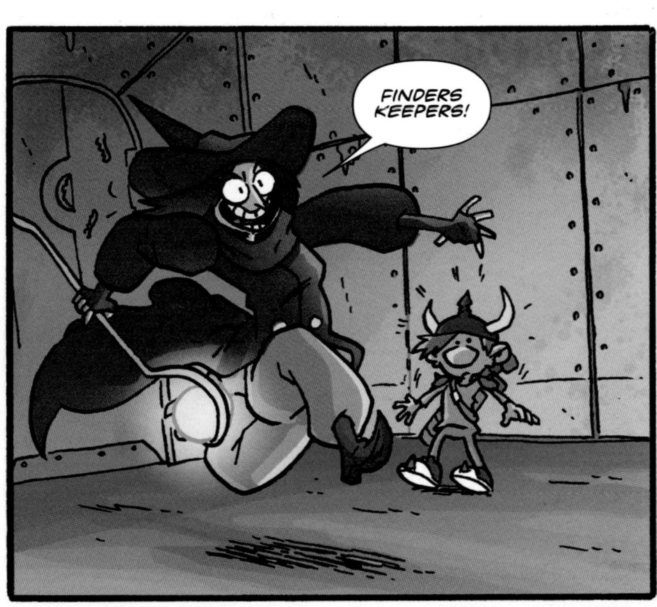
FINDERS KEEPERS!

HEY!
LEAP
ZZZAPPO

WHAT SORCERY IS THIS?
NOT MY SORCERY! NOT MY SORCERY!
THIS IS...A DUNGEON OF METAL!
PTANG
WELL LET'S MAKE THIS A DUNGEON OF FIND THE TREASURE BEFORE PIX STEALS IT!
OPEN BA-GOPEN!
SHFF
HELLO!

A MONSTER!
HEY...
NEVER SEEN THIS TYPE OF CREATURE BEFORE...
BUT WE ARE IN A DUNGEON...
AND WHEN YOU FIND SOMETHING UNEXPECTED IN A DUNGEON...
ATTACK!
AAAAAPLEASECOMETHISWAY!

INHEREPLEASE!
WE WELCOME YOU ABOARD...
EVEN MORE, WHAT SORCERY IS THIS?!
WHY DOES EVERYONE SAY THAT WHEN SOMETHING WEIRD HAPPENS?
THE STARSHIP LOVEDIAMONDS.

I AM STELLARFLEET CAPTAIN **PLACARD.**
AND THIS IS FIRST OFFICER **MITTENS.**
YOU LIVE IN THIS DUNGEON? DID **YOU** BRING US HERE?
THIS ISN'T A DUNGEON, YOU ARE ABOARD A SHIP. ONE THAT FLIES THROUGH SPACE.
IS THAT...OUR ENTIRE WORLD? WE FLY IN THE HEAVENS?!
HOW IS THIS POSSIBLE?
SPACE IS A VACUUM, SO WE'RE TECHNICALLY NOT FLYING AS THERE ISN'T ANY GRAVITY TO--
MAGIC.
WE TELEPORTED YOU HERE USING A PARTICLE RE-ORGANIZER THAT ALLOWS US TO TRANSFER MATTER--
POWERFUL MAGIC INDEED.

CAPTAIN OF THE HEAVENS, I AM **SPYKE THE FEARLESS.** THIS IS MY COLLEAGUE, THE SAGE WIZARD ADAIRE.

OH, A WIZARD? YOU'RE NOT A WITCH?
NO! I'M NOT A WITCH! I'M A **WIZARD.**
A **FEMALE!**
WIZARD!

TELL THEM YOUR FULL NAME!

ADAIRE... WITCH.
AND YOUR MIDDLE NAME.

"THE".

YOUR NAME IS **ADAIRE THE WITCH?**
MY PARENTS TRIED TO PLAN MY WHOLE LIFE OUT.
HAHAHA!

SPYKE THE FEARLESS, *HUH?* YOU SHOULD BE SPYKE THE **POOPYPANTS** AFTER THAT VAMPIRE NEST INCIDENT.
SHUTUPSHUT UPSHUTUPSHUT UPSHUTUPSHUTUP SHUTUPSHUTUP

ADVENTURERS, WE HAVE BROUGHT YOU HERE BECAUSE WE NEED YOUR HELP.
YOU WERE IN THE MIDST OF SEEKING AN ARTIFACT, CORRECT?
OH YEAH! THE TREASURE!
YOU KNOW WHERE IT IS?
OH YES. WE BROUGHT IT ON BOARD ALSO.
YOU SEE, IT BELONGS TO US.
beep beep
SHIF
BUT UPON TRANSFER, WE FOUND A SLIGHT PROBLEM.
DOUBLE SPACEPALM

YOU WERE ALL IN THE VICINITY OF THE DEVICE BUT THIS CREATURE... WELL...

EVERY TIME WE TRY TO GET...IT... OFF THE DEVICE, IT GROWLS AT US!
PRETTY SCARY!
RRRR

DON'T YOU HAVE ANY WEAPONS TO USE?

IT HAS PROVEN IMMUNE TO OUR CIVILIZATION'S ULTIMATE WEAPON...
DIPLOMACY.

JUST LIKE, WRENCH HER OFF WITH A STICK OR SOMETHING.

WELL, AS IT IS A CREATURE OF YOUR WORLD...
WE WERE HOPING YOU COULD...
SINCE YOU'RE ALREADY HERE...

I SEE HOW IT IS. YOU DON'T WANT TO GET YOUR HANDS DIRTY.

NOW, PIX, YOU WERE ALREADY ASKED NICELY TO REMOVE YOURSELF FROM THE DIAMOND...
RRRRARRGGG FFLLLFFNNG!*
*TRANSLATION: YOU IDIOTS! THESE GUYS WANT TO STEAL THE THING FOR THEMSELVES!

RRR! RRR! GGLARGHH RRRARGH!
TRANSLATION: FINDER'S KEEPERS, REMEMBER!

SO...YOU SAY THIS IS YOUR TREASURE?

THIS "TREASURE" IS NOTHING MORE THAN A SIMPLE PROBE.
LEFT BY OUR CIVILIZATION MANY YEARS AGO TO MONITOR YOUR WORLD.

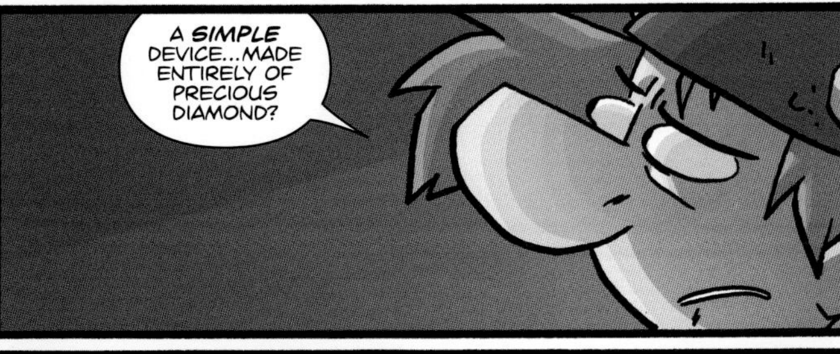
A SIMPLE DEVICE...MADE ENTIRELY OF PRECIOUS DIAMOND?

HAHA! OF COURSE! DIAMOND MUST BE RARE TO YOU!
ON OUR WORLD, WE HAVE NO NEED FOR MONEY OR MATERIAL WEALTH. DIAMOND IS ONLY VALUABLE AS AN EXTREMELY DURABLE BUILDING MATERIAL. WE USE IT FOR MANY THINGS!

SEE?
beep
clatter

WE HAVE A PROCESS WHICH ALLOWS US TO EASILY MANUFACTURE FLAWLESS DIAMONDS INTO ANY SHAPE.
DIAMONDS ARE THE BASIS OF OUR STRUCTURAL ENGINEERING, OUR SPACE EXPLORATION MANUFACTURE, THE CLOTHES WE WEAR.

IN FACT, EVEN MY FACE IS DIAMOND.

WAIT, WHAT?

THAT STATEMENT'S GOING TO NEED SOME EXPLANATION...
ARE YOU SAYING THAT YOUR FACE IS *MADE* OF DIAMOND...OR THAT YOU CONSIDER YOUR FACE TO *BE A* DIAMOND?

OH, PLEASE DON'T GET HIM STARTED, IT'S A TOUCHY SUBJECT.

VERY WELL! I HAVE DEVISED A PLAN TO RID YOU OF THIS CREATURE.
HEY, I'M UP, I'M UP!
BUT I ASK THAT YOU PLEASE STEP OUTSIDE FOR A MOMENT AS MY COLLEAGUE AND I TAKE CARE OF THIS...NASTY BUSINESS.
GLRK!
WON'T TAKE LONG!
shove
shove
shff
CRASH!
BANG BANG!
ZAP!
ZZZAPP!
SO. HOW ABOUT THEM DIAMONDVILLE DIAMONDS?
YEP. LIKE 'EM.
LIKE THOSE DIAMONDS.

AAAND...
DONE!

PHEW! THERE YOU GO!

IT IS DONE?
DID YOU HAVE TO...

YUP! YUP! HAD TO BE DONE.
A SHAME, SURE, BUT SHE WON'T BE BOTHERING *YOU* AGAIN!

IT IS INDEED... A SHAME...WE STRIVE TO BE EXPLORERS. NOT DESTROYERS.

SOOOOO...

ZZZAPPO
DID IT WORK? DID IT WORK?
THEY'RE GONE! YOU WERE ABLE TO CRAWL THROUGH THE SMALL TUNNELS!
YEAH! I SENT 'EM BACK TO THE SURFACE OF THE PLANET!

YOU WERE ABLE TO LEARN THE SHIP'S GREAT MAGICS SO QUICKLY?
HA! YEAH! WHEN I SAW THEY TRANSPORTED US SO FAR, I FIGURED THERE MUST BE A DEVICE THAT CAN TRANSMIT MATERIAL AT BASE-LEVEL AND THAT IT MUST BE ACTIVATED IN THE CONTROL CENTER--
YES. GREAT MAGICS.

PIX! DO YOU THINK YOU CAN TAKE US TO THIS DIAMOND WORLD THE CAPTAIN SPOKE OF?
I'M WORKIN' ON IT.
MAYBE HE FELT HIS FACE WAS AS SMOOTH AS A DIAMOND...
NEVER MIND THAT! WITH THIS SHIP, THE RICHES OF THE HEAVENS ARE OURS FOR THE TAKING!
HEHEH. DON'T COUNT ON IT...
SUBJECTS LOCKED: 2
TELEPORT
HUH?
WHA?
HUH? I DIDN'T SAY ANYTHING.
-END-

AFTER COUNTLESS DELVES INTO DANK DUNGEONS OF DOUR DARKNESS, ISN'T IT TIME FOR A CHANGE?
?
MUNCHKIN
Story by Jim Zub
Art by Rian Sygh
THE OPEN WATER BECKONS AND WE MUST ANSWER ITS SIREN SONG!
YES! ADVENTURE, SALTY SEA WATER, AND PIRACY!
WOO HOO!
No, no, not stealin' stuff on the internet piracy. We mean 'OP'--Original Piracy!
JUST A BOAT, SOME LOYAL SHIPMATES, MAYBE A PACKAGE OF SHARK JERKY AND...
...AND...UH...
OKAY, THIS WHOLE "WAVES ROCKING BACK AND FORTH" THING IS A BIT MUCH.
HEH.
COULD WE MAYBE SLOW IT DOWN A BIT? IT'S KINDA--

BAAAAARF!

RIGHT, THEN. LET'S SEE WHICH ACCENTS WILL BE REPRESENTED BY OUR INFAMOUS MUNCHKIN CAP'NS.
OI, OI.
HOI, HOI.
OUI, OUI.
HOLA, HOLA.
A RUM-SOAKED CREW OF HARDY SAILORS AND A SWIFT SHIP AWAITS THE CAP'N WHO CAN PROVE THEIR WAVE WORTHINESS IN OUR MUNCHKIN BOOTY CONTEST.
TEST 1: THE INTERVIEW
FAVORITE FOOD?
PEANUT BUTTER AND JELLYFISH SANDWICHES.
FAVORITE COLOR?
AAAARANGE.

TEST 2: WARDROBE FITTING
HOLE $1
SO, WHAT'LL IT BE? WOODEN LEG OR HOOK HAND?
UHHH...
HOW MUCH FOR THE EARRINGS?
THEY'RE A BUCK-AN-EAR, OF COURSE.

TEST 3: SWORD SKILLS
COACH
sigh

TEST 4: MARINE IDENTIFICATION
CATFISH.
DOGFISH.
FISHFISH.

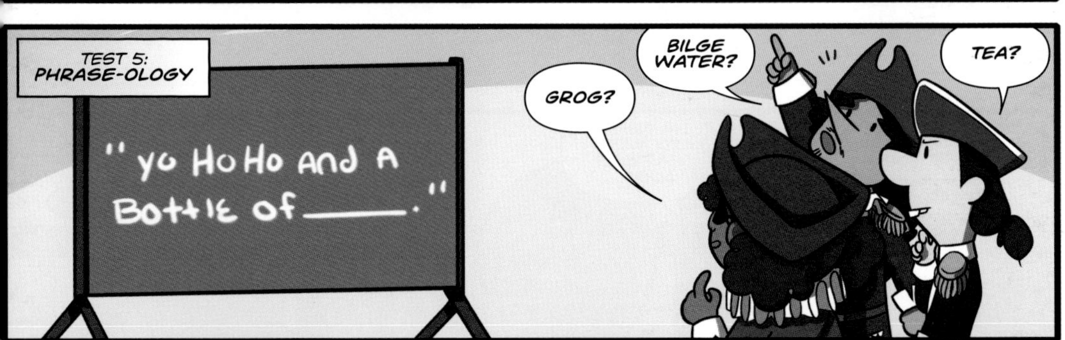
TEST 5: PHRASE-OLOGY
"Yo Ho Ho and a Bottle of ____."
GROG?
BILGE WATER?
TEA?

TEST 6: SHIP ANATOMY
PORT.
STARBOARD.
POOP DECK.

TEST 7: PLANK WALKING
REALLY?

TEST 8: CANNON CLEANING
Psssssh

TEST 9: SCRATCH A SCURVY DOG
THIS IS LESS THAN FLEA-SING.

TEST 10: DUEL WITH PRIVATEARS
I'M TRYING TO AVOID EARRING LOSS...

TEST 11: MILK A SEA COW
I DARE SAY, THIS IS UDDERLY EMBARRASSING.

TEST 12: THE FINE ART OF SHARKING
SO, YOU ALL IN, OR WHAT?
GULP

AND NOW, THE **ENDURANCE** ROUND!
CROSS HAUL THE MIZZENBRACE!
CAREEN THE FUTTOCK-SHROUDS!
SPLICE THE FORECASTLE!
BELAY THE AFT TOPGALLANTS!
NICE WORK, CAP'NS!
YOU'RE REALLY SHOWING US YOUR FINEST SHIP **SHAPES.**

AND NOW, AT LAST, THE FINAL TEST: DEFEAT THE DANGEROUS DAVY JONES!
HEY, HOW'S IT GOIN'?

AHHUUUGH!
AHHHH!

LOOKS LIKE YOU WIN AGAIN, DAVY.
AHHHHHHHHHHH
GEEZ, THAT WAS ANTICLIMACTIC.
I DIDN'T EVEN GET TA KEELHAUL ANYBODY.

LOOKS LIKE ALL THE SAILORS RAN AWAY TOO.
THAT'S OKAY.
I'M USED TA HAVIN' A SKELETON CREW.

ANYONE SEEN MY LOCKER ANYWHERE? I KEEP LOSIN' IT...
-END-

"TABLE OF CONTENTS"
BY JOHN KOVALIC
?
?
HEY! LARD-BUTTS! OUTTA THE WAY! COMIN' THROUGH!

MOVE IT, MEAT PUPPETS! VERY IMPORTANT COUNTER ON THE MOVE! FRIGHTENING FURNITURE WITH PLACES TO GO! DEMONIC FURNISHING WITH PEOPLE TO TO SEE!
YEARRRRRRGH!
SPLINTER! SMASH!
SPLINTER SPLINTER SPLINTER
BREAK! CLEAVE! WREND!
CARVE! HACK! SAW!

PUFF
PUFF
PANT
TWITCH
TWITCH
TWITCH

I HATE WANDERING MONSTER TABLES...
Kovalic

COVER GALLERY

Issue 1 Cover by
Ian McGinty
Colors by Fred Stresing

Issue 1 Jackpot Cover by
Evan Palmer

Issue 1 Cover by
Tyler Jenkins

ISSUE 1 BOOM! TEN YEARS VARIANT COVER BY
SHELLI PAROLINE & BRADEN LAMB

10

Issue 1 Variant Cover by

John Kovalic

Colors by Melissa Kaercher

Issue 1 BOOM! Studios Exclusive Cover by
Daniel Bayliss

Issue 1 Second Print Cover by
Ian McGinty
Colors by Fred Stresing

Issue 1 JetPack Comics Exclusive Cover by
Wren McDonald

ISSUE 1 EMERALD CITY COMICON EXCLUSIVE COVER BY
PAUL MAYBURY

SIDDELL • ZUB • HOLMES • SYGH • STRESING
MUNCHKIN
PAUL MAYBURY 2015
IN SEATTLE

Issue 2 Cover by
Ian McGinty
Colors by Fred Stresing

Issue 2 Variant Cover by
Tyler Crook

Issue 2 BOOM! Studios Exclusive Cover by
Daniel Bayliss

Issue 2 Seond Print Cover by
Stefan Tosheff

Issue 2 JetPack Comics Exclusive Cover by
Rian Sygh

Issue 3 Cover by
Ian McGinty
Colors by Fred Stresing

Issue 3 Variant Cover by
Chris Schweizer

ISSUE 3 BOOM! STUDIOS EXCLUSIVE COVER BY
DANIEL BAYLISS

Issue 4 Cover by
Ian McGinty
Colors by Fred Stresing

ISSUE 4 VARIANT COVER BY
EVAN PALMER

Issue 4 BOOM! Studios Exclusive Cover by
Daniel Bayliss

Issue 1 BOOM! Studios Exclusive Card

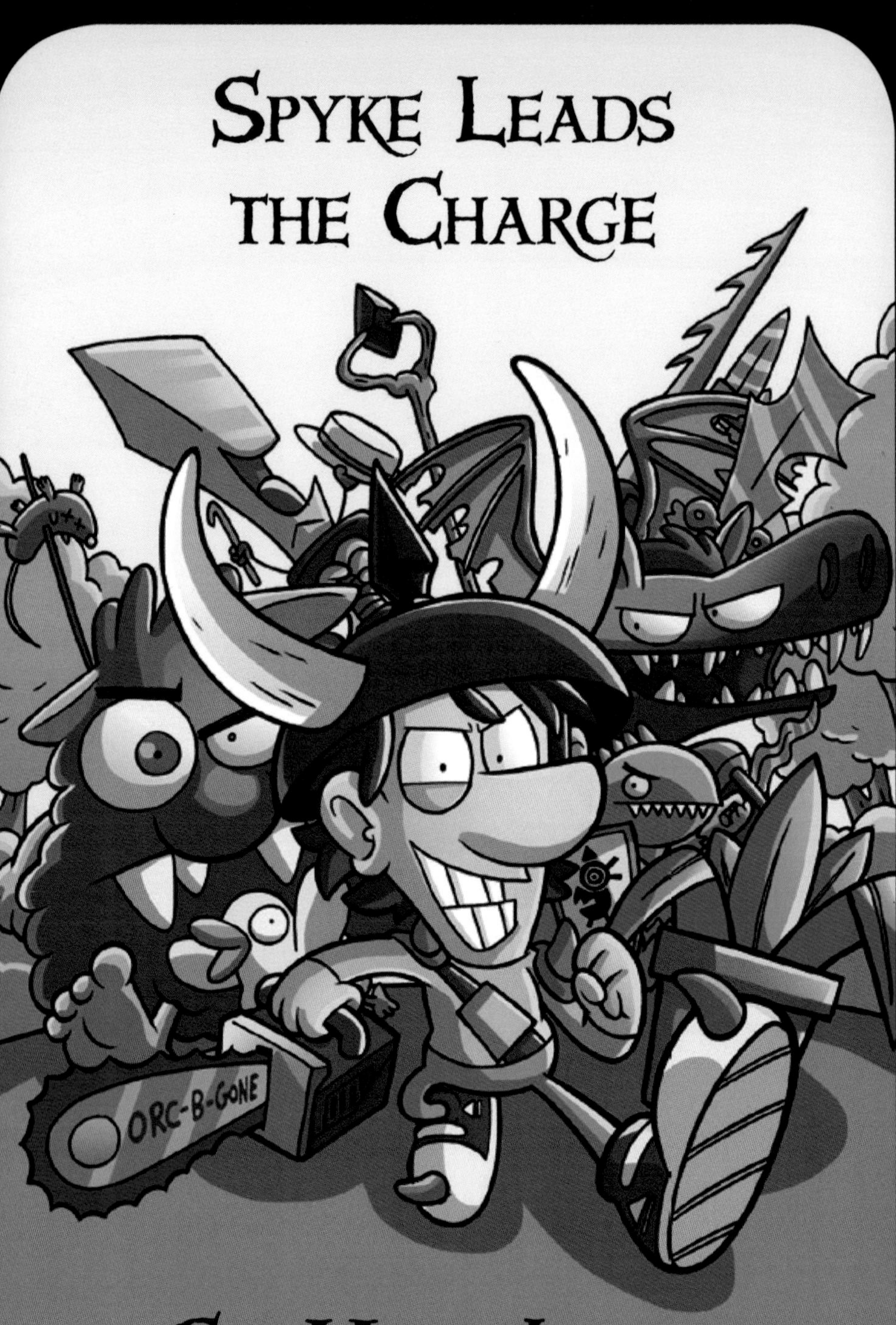

Go Up a Level

munchkin.sjgames.com

BOOM! BOX

ISSUE 2 BOOM! STUDIOS EXCLUSIVE CARD

SUPER HOARD!

Play at any time on your turn except during combat.

Discard all the Treasure cards in your hand, then draw that many plus one more. Then put this card on the bottom of the Treasure discards.

munchkin.sjgames.com

BOOM! BOX™

SELL YOUR LEVELS FOR ITEMS

At any time on your turn except during combat, you may trade one or more of your levels for Items from the Treasure discards totalling up to 1,000 Gold Pieces per level.

Put this card back in the box after you make the trade – it's out of the game!

Boom Box

Play during any combat. +4 to either side. Usable once only.

munchkin.sjgames.com